THE TEN SYMPHONIES OF GORKA KÖNIG

A Fictional Textbook

ALSO BY IAN DALLAS:

IAN DALLAS

THE TEN SYMPHONIES OF GORKA KÖNIG

A Fictional Textbook

BUDGATE PRESS

First edition: Kegan Paul International, 1989
This edition 2013
All rights reserved
budgate@gmail.com

Budgate Press
Postnet Suite 402
Constantia 7848
Cape Town
Republic of South Africa

ISBN: 978-0-620-46513-7
Printed by Lightning Source

CONTENTS

τὰ ... μεγάλα πάντα ἐπισφαλῆ

'All great things stand in peril.'

Plato: *Republic.*

Introduction

My original intention had been to write a musical study of the symphonic works of Gorka König. The more I tried to write about König musicologically the more I realized that it was impossible to discuss his work without describing his life. Yet since so much of his life was lived out in the realm of ideas it meant, in turn, that I could not avoid the intellectual forces that drove him in his lifelong quest, for his symphonies were in a way the summary statements of his whole existence and philosophy.

In delving deeper into his life, issues of political import and controversy mixed with concepts which, while not difficult to define, were not at all in line with popular thinking today. Since König himself experienced tremendous resistance to his thinking on certain matters, and felt that a current version of events, and indeed reality, had effectively barred people from access to understanding the motor forces of history and to philosophical discourse itself, I have found it necessary to repeat in various forms the same concepts throughout this text in the hope that this repetition will clarify the issues through looking at them from slightly altered perspectives. For this I must beg the reader's patience, for while his reaction may be to feel that a theme has been stated earlier, let the reader also recall that these same subjects are not generally permitted in the current public discourse which is itself remarkably circumscribed. As König's wife once wrote: 'If only one point of view is tolerated as reality we are dealing with a psychosis not basic reality.' What has to be decided is whether König could express themes of universal significance and profound humanity while holding views which were contrary to such a stance. He himself has consciously insisted that this is not possible, and further, that a man's creativity and his life are inseparable.

It has proved impossible to write of his music without taking on these profound and often disturbing theses which so passionately concerned him in his lifetime and must clearly be involved in his final public act, his disappearance. The disappearance of Gorka König and his wife after such an active and triumphantly successful, if controversial, life surely lies outside the realm of musical theory and analysis. Yet after the Tenth Symphony there is an inescapable symmetry in what followed: after his ultimate musical statement, his departure to an unknown destination, and thus his silence. It is the silence of Gorka König which now speaks so powerfully to the world, forcing us to listen to what he had to say – and what he had to say is to be heard not only in his music but in his life and his philosophy. Nietzsche said: 'The end of a melody is not its goal, but nonetheless, if the melody had not reached its end it would not have reached its goal either.' With the ten symphonies of Gorka König we can be in no doubt that the composer had completed his melody and achieved his goal.

Chapter One

Gorka Konig: His Life

1.

Gorka König once said, 'The trouble with me is that I've been famous all my life.' Born of famous parents he had not left childhood before he himself had become more famous. He was born in 1920 just outside Zurich; his father, Johann König, was then at the height of his activity as a philosopher, while his mother, Anna Sorenson, had just abandoned her youthful triumphs in classical theatre to take on a new and glamorous role of film star.

Perhaps something has to be said about this period of his childhood not for reasons of psychological interpretation but rather in order to indicate the intellectual and social milieu which later certainly produced a profound resonance in the composer, so that we might say that he reproduced inwardly and often around him that same ambience of study and expression that he had grown up in, both in his early years in Switzerland and then later in his teens in the effulgent energy of the new Third Reich.

It was just at the time Gorka was born that two elements in his father's intellectual activity came together. On the one hand he made his shift from being the leader of the neo-Kantians to embarking on his series of works on existential psychology that was to ensure his place forever in the philosophical pantheon, and on the other hand, and very much part of that shift, he had participated in the cabaret movement that swept the intellectuals of Europe, writing material for singers and comedians who appeared in famous night-spots, like the Cabaret Voltaire and the Jiki, along with new poets of Dadaism and other negative anarchist strands which inspired that strange time so full of portents of a storm to come.

So it was that while his father brought together in his person two utterly alien worlds, the world of natural philosophy and the world of existential satire, his mother brought together the world of classical theatre and the glittering new personalities of the cinema. To the young Gorka it may have meant little that the knee he was dandled on was that of the grim theologian Karl Barth, or that the lap he threw up on belonged to the actor Emil Jannings, but as his personality began to emerge, as he entered his teens and his young soul began to search for its own nature and its own manner he found that the people around him were themselves experts at the very elements he desired to take on, the qualities he sought – cards of identity were presented and shuffled and dealt with stunning verbal and theatrical panache – so that very quickly he learned to dissemble, to bluff, to change position, to survive. He was among experts and there is little doubt that the games he played in that exalted company he repeated with sophisticated variations in his adult life. This is not to deny the authenticity of his character but to indicate how cunningly he had learned to draw a complex maze that led others away from his own minotaur.

Looking back on that time it seems unfair, and a mark of the world's jealousy of beautiful women, especially beautiful and talented women, that the family's social circle was known as Sorenson's Circus. The truth is that the main group who frequented the König's villa were friends of her husband, what she called 'that unmixable mix' of philosophers and entertainers. Her friends, who were mostly actors, seemed, as actors tend to be, always on their best behaviour, unsure of their own social standing and anxious to be accepted, never able to adopt the raucous ease of the aristocratic philosophers or able to equal them in downright rudeness or anarchic fun.

Unfortunately the circle which was so alluring to the press and the avid magazine readers of the time presented to its central characters, the Königs, a constant source of conflict, alienation, and divided loyalties. As he grew up it inevitably seemed to the young Gorka that in some way he had to choose 'which side he was on', for the two sets that made up the König Set all in the end participated in the König War, the endless squabbling and disapproving and loyalty testing that the two main protagonists put their friends through in a kind of extension of their own bid for supremacy of identity, fame, and simple domestic authority. In all this Gorka had no doubt that his mother was the wronged party, but what the wrong was his child's mind could never have expressed – some kind of betrayal of feelings, forgotten anniversaries and birthdays, non-appearances at dinners that 'mattered' to mother, being excluded from events that in turn 'mattered' to father. He had decided that the simple truth was that for all the tensions and tantrums and crises that shook the temperamental household, mother was not to blame, Johann König, the 'great' philosopher had to be held responsible. In the end the message was clear, it was that his greatness had been inescapably imprisoned in pejorative inverted commas, he was not to his household what he was to the world. Thus, for Gorka, the first ingredient of a powerful neurosis had fallen into place among the after-dinner games, the idyllic picnics and the Socratic dialogues under the alpine firs.

In this world of totally incomprehensible philosophical discourse combined with deliciously easy charades and songs of cabaret artists and actors, the son of the famous couple soon began to make his allegiances. Childhood illnesses shuttled him between the private schools around the city and a series of dubious tutors but the key factor of these years was that more and more he took refuge in the inner circle of his mother's friends, learning their secret language, adopting their latest turn of phrase with a sophistication that enchanted his listeners mixed as it was with a naïve failure to grasp its true innuendo. At the same time the growing child became a burden to the vivacious and glamorous actress with her quite intense ambition to conquer the silver screen. She did not like to be too much associated with the role of mother, although a few adoring pictures in the press of prestigious König Christmasses with little Gorka unwrapping his presents were a good thing. Apart from that in her social life outside the König villa Anna Sorenson soon looked eagerly for a means to 'get rid of' the unwelcome child whose every year diminished her 'eternal youth'.

It was a visit by a renowned pianist, she later claimed it was the young Claudio Arrau but the dates do not bare this out, that triggered the moment that set Gorka on his career in music. Let us allow the composer himself to recount the event, for his version is highly significant for all that follows:

'The truth is that the music did not interest me at all, for I could not understand it. The boy playing the piano seemed to me most unpleasant and I noticed he made terrible faces while he played as if the whole matter were, to him, a torment. He went on and on, people tutted, there was a general air of amazement, and slowly but surely it dawned on me that they were not listening to the music, they were watching the pianist. It was his doing it, his achievement, whether it was technical or prodigious, or olympic, I only knew that it was his doing it, his attack on the black and white keys, his leaning over the keyboard, his memory which never faltered, his command, his mastery that held them in thrall. 'When he finished there was the usual burst of applause that was meted out to artists, speakers, singers, all the circus who came to my house. But it had always been for the work, the thing, but now they crowded round the obnoxious little fellow saying – 'He's a genius, he is a new someone-or-other, he will be the master of the age.'

'I recall once in Seville after a bullfight as I sat with Juan Belmonte in his grimly dignified club on the Sierpes he told me that he decided to be a bullfighter the day he had seen the neighbours running through the streets weeping and calling out, 'So-and-so the torero has been killed by the bull!' And it was then he decided to take on that deadly dangerous art just to be loved that much, no, just to matter that much to another human being.

'And so, I that night, slipping out the back of the music room climbed up to my bedroom, locked the door and knelt down to speak to God, for although I studiously avoided my mother's catholicism and my father's incomprehensible protestantism, I always kept up a lively conversation with God, for He was clearly responsible for creating existence in my, I guess, neo-Kantian mind. I informed Him that I intended to be a world-renowned pianist – then paused, for I did not want to turn into

the spoiled brat I had observed downstairs –
unless, that is, He came up with something
better. I gave Him three days and nothing
proposed itself so I asked my mother to let me
begin piano lessons. And so it was that I entered
the world of music.'

The success of Gorka König from his first pro-
fessional concert was complete. Even allowing
for the inevitable publicity, the almost cloying
loyalty of the press, the parental reputation, purely
as a musical event the König child was hailed
as an authentic prodigy. The Zurich public had
never been reputed to lack critical acumen, but
equally they are renowned for their generosity in
enthusiasm and at his first recital he was called
back again and again to enchant a glittering
audience. Overnight Gorka König had won what
he sought, total attention. For a brief spell it
seemed that his mother had discovered him as if
for the first time. They became 'friends', they were
photographed together, they travelled together,
the trick had succeeded. The photographs of the
time still evoke a romantic dated image of mother
and child, her bobbed hair tousled and her profile
carefully presented to the lens, his long pianist's
locks held in place by his favourite Basque beret
which he wore in honour of his name throughout
his life. The fact was that his success as a concert

pianist arrived just at the right moment for Anna Sorenson and the wave of sympathetic publicity that followed the renowned mother-and-son duo also helped launch her with a new cinema public that was more sophisticated and at the same time more identified with its stars.

There are no recordings of Gorka's efforts as a concert pianist but the critics all agree that he was technically impeccable, and it was this almost scientific capacity to give readings of the music that impressed the serious public – for there seems very rarely to be much in the way of an interpretation from a child performer – and which kept them waiting for those first signs of maturity that would add to this technical brilliance some depths, some personal feeling, a voice.

Finally, with the emergence of his own sexual identity and with the inevitable crisis of adolescence, came a quality in the piano playing that seemed to justify what had until then been a kind of popular adulation due more to the mother than to the son. This new element in his playing did not simply present itself as an improvement but rather it came with a completely new repertoire, and that change in his concert material provided the vehicle for his new-found self-expression. Gorka König discovered Franz Liszt, not the popular Liszt of the concert hall but the complex, reflective, one might almost say philosophical Liszt, the Liszt of the 'Années de Pèlerinage'. Whether he saw these long reflective works as if they were musical commentaries on his own life or whether he tasted for the first time the secret transmutation that turned deep personal thoughts, feelings and, yes, experience, into the coded language of music will never be known. Yet the perceptive student of König could well date the awakening of the composer's consciousness, of the composer-identity from the encounter with the masterly Liszt studies, still so little known, still so little played, precisely because of their intense inwardness, their astonishing modernity, their economy of expression, their utterly unromantic intimacy.

Surely it was this encounter with Franz Liszt at his most intimate, his most alone, his most personal, that first made Gorka König aware that one could say all these painful things about life and loneliness and just the difficult matter of being alive. He said in one of his letters 'the sheer difficulty of existence that remains to those of us who have rejected categorically the option of suicide'. Whether or not this was the case we can only surmise, but it was the impact of these Liszt recitals of the travel studies that brought with it an invitation to perform in Vienna. And it was there in the musical capital of Europe that, from a historical point of view, the young pianist at the age of fifteen turned into the composer who was to speak to the whole world in a way they would never forget, speak of their struggle with his voice so that it seemed to be his struggle and their voice. The man who opened the door of composition to the adolescent genius was the aloof and aristocratic master of the most absolute inwardness, Anton von Webern.

The Königs held a reception to let the notoriously snobbish Viennese musical circles meet their son before the concert. It was there that the reclusive master put in a brief appearance, promised to attend the recital and disappeared. But they had met. They had shaken hands, bowed formally as two men meeting and exchanged a few words. For Gorka König, however, that in itself was enough. He knew – he recognized his 'other', his creative self appeared clearly in the mirror of the master's face. There and then, in front of the whole world of music assembled under the Königs' roof he declared in a firm already broken voice, 'I am going to be a composer.' Then, as if not satisfied with the impact that this had made on the guests, for to him it was everything, he added, 'This will be my last recital.' And in case that was still not enough he added with boyish glee, 'I hate the piano.'

The farewell performance of a fifteen-year-old prodigy with a repertoire of mature and introspective music was too much for the sentimental Viennese. A black market developed for the tickets, the night turned into the social event of the season and it seemed that all Vienna had turned out as if, by its post-Hapsburgian responsibility, it had taken upon itself the job of persuading the young genius to return to his instrument, because they loved him. Whatever it was, that contact, that affection, like the bond between the Sevillians and the dead torero, sparked into vivid life that night in the Vienna concert hall. He played not for them but for his new hero, his master, his mirror, the remote and melancholy composer that he now longed to be. They were moved to their hearts, they called him again and again, after the inescapable and seemingly endless recalls he gave one farewell wave and called out in a little voice that seemed so thin in the suddenly silent air of the concert hall, 'Goodbye!' And to calls of 'No! No!' Gorka König walked off the stage, his triumphal life as a pianist over. His new life – undefined, unknown, just an intention and an adolescent recognition of genius, a genius that he was convinced belonged essentially to him.

He did not see Webern that night at the tumultuous reception that followed his concert. He stood alone, pathetic and lost at one moment, and at another surrounded by admiring and babbling groups proffering their invitations – to Salzburg, to Berlin, to the Alps, to the lakes, to the palace, anywhere to be the centre of their jaded attention. Finally, the young musician, realising that of course he would not come, and that it was perfectly fitting that he did not come, went alone upstairs to bed and immediately fell asleep.

He had to wait several days before his adolescent pride, his spoiled König prodigality would humble itself to write the obligatory begging letter. He knew it was the price of apprenticeship and when he finally wrote it he managed a blend of youthful sincerity and the nearest thing he could manage to pleading and then he added just that something, a phrase, a word, an idea that touched the heart of the composer, or perhaps it was the mixture of poetic humility and youthful clumsiness that made Webern relent. A message came instructing him to visit Dr. Webern the next morning.

Nobody knows what happened that historic morning but it remained imprinted on the mind of Gorka König with such force that at different times he told the story differently. Very often when an event has made a deep impact on the soul, the intellect reviews it and each time finds a new and essential element, or the imagination even embellishes the event with a fantasy and yet that fantasy is itself an intrinsic part of the truth of that moment and its meaning, so that it is like a diamond with many facets, having lights from its own structure as well as different refracted lights that illuminate it now one way and later another. Such was the first encounter of master and pupil in a relationship that was brief, profound, and the ineluctable core of the musical identity of a man all but totally the opposite of his mentor.

In a letter to his father recalling Webern's tragic death, or murder, as he insisted on calling it, he wrote of their first meeting: 'That day he hardly spoke to me. My mind was full of his Opus 24 Concerto and so it came as a shock to me when he finally faced me and said, sternly, glaring at me from his pince-nez which were so curved that instead of his eyes I saw only light, "Wagner!" I repeated the name both incredulously, and at the same time with something of the awe with which he had imbued that most emotional of names. "You have no choice. Go back to where it all ended. Start from there." He repeated, "You have no choice."'

Perhaps it is worth also quoting the other word of advice that he was given, if it was advice, or perhaps we should see it more as the kind of oracular message that profoundly reflective men do indulge in communicating to children who are theoretically too young to understand. König is reported to have said that as they were taking leave Webern held the boy for a moment and said to him: "Germany! Never forget it has a secret. Not this – not politics. This Austria, it will be Germany – this is another matter. I mean Kant and Beethoven, Wagner and Nietzsche, Bach and Luther – Germany. Remember."

The story has never been verified and of course it was later to play a very significant role in the building up of a political character for König, one which is in itself a kind of judgment on him, or it should be said against him, as if the idea of having a good opinion of Germany had during the century become some kind of crime, or that no good opinion could be voiced without betraying the deep humanism which was its greatest contribution not only through philosophy but through music and a depth of spirit that remained unique to it, denied or not. Again, if Webern did not say it, it is as if he said it or should have said it or would have said it or König would have desired it from him or had perceived it in him. What we know Gorka wrote in a letter to his father was: 'They killed him – for being himself, for being great, and for being German!'

Whatever transpired there, one result is indisputable. From that very day Gorka König became a composer. He did not wait for instruction and for theory to start setting down his musical ideas. In the tradition of Beethoven he wrote down every phrase or idea that came to him in a musical notebook, like Beethoven's too, sometimes jotting down melodies of the utmost banality but which with the subtlest adjustment could become transformed – as later they were into the deeply felt and ravishing musical language of the great symphonies.

It was as though he had been storing up inside him a whole range of feelings and forms and curves of sound that he wanted now to come out of him and they did, gushing and turbulent like one of the alpine streams that turn into torrential cataracts. The ice had broken. The detached and good boy, the well-mannered, likeable gifted son on show to the world of culture in comfortable and sedate Zurich, became overnight the immersed scholar, the studious bore. It was as if from the moment that he began studying musical theory he ceased to have any life at all. His routine of meals and outings was shattered. He became the obsessive student, his nose forever buried in a book. He ate on the move, sandwiches, a coffee. He never read another menu, but took what was put in front of him. He did not become boorish where once he had been sensitive, but rather he became absent-minded, withdrawn, not interested in anything except acquiring the necessary education to permit him to say those things he was convinced it was his duty now to say, though what they were he did not know and from where they would come he could not tell. He was like a prisoner desperately trying to learn Morse code in time to send out a signal begging for his liberation before his execution.

And while he saw his studies as a profoundly urgent rush against time, the world outside also hurtled with growing speed towards a series of events that already by 1935 suggested to some people an imminent crash. It is important at this juncture to mention the lives of his influential parents who up until that point had held the child in thrall, partly through the natural role of parenthood but more importantly through their roles as leaders of a certain circle or set of people who were in the mainstream of the cultural and intellectual life of their time.

On their return from Vienna the Königs, now with a young son committed to being a composer, were already at a crossroads in their marriage. They had survived the economic troubles of the stock-market collapse that had made such an impact in

America and later reverberated through Europe, but their own private life being so interwoven with the age they lived in, not by way of background, but because it was the language in which they expressed their intellectual existence, found itself in the same kind of crisis. More and more at odds with each other, the conservative and academic Johann saw himself presented as an opponent not only to the world of, but to the existence of, his wife. Anna Sorenson had come to identity herself with the theatre of social comment and satire, lightly but pointedly and with increasing accuracy hitting the targets of corruption and conflict that were the themes of the day. Abandoning her aspirations as a film star she had returned to the world of cabaret and sketches, the radical world of theatrical social critique. Brecht was her idol and she saw that Zurich was not a place where her outspoken views would find a public.

At the same time Johann König saw himself making his definitive break with the scientific calm of the post-Kantians and taking his place once and for all with that other stream, the existential school, and while he claimed that this did not imply a break but rather a jump, such metaphors by their physical crudity underlined to others that he was aware that there was no going back from his change in position and if he did it would never be forgiven in academic circles. It had about it the most uncomfortable confirmation of every existentialist's view of life, implying about it just such a leap, such an abyss, that he felt furious he was unable to present his new position as one having been reached after the utmost analysis, after the most objective and clinical examination, after the most effective rejection of an inadequate vocabulary for the adoption of a more authentic one. Authentic! he still did not like the word's unscientific ring, as if he had been convinced or worse, converted, to the existential argument rather than, as he insisted, he had been able to demonstrate that this was the culminating act of the reasoning mind facing the incomprehensible universe. 'Facing' still had a dramatic feel about it and he realized that he had shed the clear terminology of the Kantian tradition for the dangerous world of metaphor, meaning, and, God help him, poetry. He shuddered. Aristotle's methodology was one thing, but risking the Platonic slide area of concepts and vision was another thing.

In order to submit his new thinking to the most rigorous discipline he decided to move to Freiburg, long the capital of the South-West School of Axiological Kantianism. He would not take a post there, he decided. There was none anyhow, and he was, frankly, intellectually suspect simply because he was so popular, an unforgivable trait in a philosopher. Falling down wells, going mad, or just being ignored until dead, was considered the proper fate for a formal philosopher, not popularity with people who should not know what you are talking about, let alone what you mean. The Königs arrived in Freiburg to much publicity, not all of which Johann was sure he understood – why should people be so interested in the arrival in a small provincial if prestigious, university town, of a Kantian edging towards existential psychology? Anna Sorenson was convinced she knew exactly why they were interested. Did this mean that the Königs were throwing in their lot with the new and powerful regime that had swept aside the decadent and hopeless Weimar Republic? Anna Sorenson knew from their first day in Freiburg that while Johann could accept and work with what he found there she could not. Saturated in the language and critique of the Brechtians and the cabaret-radicals she saw herself entering an alien world which would have no place for her glamour, her allure, her sophistication mixed with political toughness. The day she arrived she began her preparations to leave for America – her Brechtian loyalty did not extend to offering her services to the chilly theatres of Moscow.

Gorka König hardly noticed the move. He was able to continue his musical studies in this new town and whatever the impact of the increasing rift between his parents he never showed it or expressed it to anyone. Others still believed that the charmed König family remained attractive and fascinating, with the two antagonists always haloed by the light of their reputations and the gifted boy so full of their golden promise.

Gorka, who had always thought of himself as Swiss, and German as his language, now immersed himself in being German, following the counsel of his master, the Viennese doctor. Just at the point that a deeper divide might have opened between parents and child aggravated by the individuation of adolescence, he found a new interest in them for having turned out to be proper Germans. In 1935 in Freiburg being German was at last and again something for which a man could be profoundly grateful. After the degradations that followed the world war and the horrific anarchy of the almost successful communist revolution, the so-called Republic had pulled the country down into a seemingly bottomless pit of shame. The child brothels, the notorious sexual mores, the fabulous inflation, the starvation, all that social squalor had been in a few short years swept away and already the German spirit was awakening and its industry and technological genius was beginning to express itself again. In 1935, in Freiburg, in those early years of the Third Reich, Gorka König was gloriously happy.

2.

At the end of 1937 König moved out of his student lodgings and set up an apartment with the intention of starting work on his first major musical composition. A fellow university student moved in with him and for those who see importance in these things her name was Ann and she was studying philosophy. He spoke to no-one about his composition, and whatever she knew went with her into the grave when she was killed during the war by British bombers.

In 1938 he completed the composition and pre-pared for its first public performance. The public interest, of course, was enormous. His father was accepted by the national government, his mother was viewed most dubiously, but was protected by her distinguished husband's reputation. At the same time it was known that the young Gorka had openly declared Webern as his master and, as one of the New Vienna School, Webern was considered along with his own mentor, Shoenberg, as a cultural bolshevik. There was no doubt that a piece in the manner of the proscribed decadence would receive an icy welcome. When the Freiburg first performance took place before a public uncertain of what they should expect from the son of such controversial parents the impact was somehow all the more overwhelming.

No-one expected or could have been prepared for what they heard that night – from the moment the audience opened their programmes and saw the title the place tingled with anticipation: The Wagner Symphony by Gorka König. From having expected a twelve-tone essay in mathematical method they anticipated the very opposite as the conductor took the podium, a lush tribute to the 'seamless web of sound' of the genius of Bayreuth. What they heard was neither, what they heard was a new and original voice, in clear and masterly command both of form and feeling. When the famous final cord reverberated through the hall and died in shimmering and diminishing sound there followed a breath-taking silence and then the hall erupted into a roar of adulation and approval.

A month later the symphony had been requested by the Munich civic authorities as the climax of a three-day Festival which was to be attended by the Führer. König was to receive the ultimate accolade of his nation, his symphonic statement about Wagner was to be performed in front of Germany's most famous Wagnerian, the Chancellor himself.

It was this honour, which was the first success, indeed triumph, of Gorka König that precipitated the crisis that had been brewing in the König household. For the civic honour to be paid for the artistic triumph of their son, which had in itself eclipsed their fame, meant at the same time that as proud and dutiful German parents the elder Königs would have to stand approvingly behind Gorka to receive the accolade of acceptance from Adolf Hitler himself. The point of view of his father was critical detachment mingled with a streak of envy which he was much too honest with himself to deny. Anxious not to be motivated with generational meanness he leaned to the public commitment implied in the Munich meeting. His mother had no doubts – the matter involved no personal motivation – it was clear to her that her offspring was a genius, had she not always said so, and would it not always be so – for that he needed no approval from the state. The issue was political – and she was not going to stand meekly behind her son, in a white neo-Greek Chanel dinner gown with her shingled blonde hair, the perfect Aryan mother, and confirm the doctrines of a politique she loathed. While her husband grudgingly admitted to himself envy of his son, Anna Sorenson grudgingly admitted to herself that her inescapable political position meant she would never meet the Führer, and the knowledge of this attraction made her all the more vehement in her opposition. It became no more simply a matter of her refusal to attend the Festival but of her refusal to permit the encounter to take place at all. She stood out firmly for a boycott of the event. They, the Königs, must refuse to attend, and he must withdraw his symphony from public performance in Germany and take it to the waiting public of Paris and New York.

To Gorka's parents this was familiar territory — personal battle and intimate animosity played out in the language of political conflict — they had thrived on it all their lives, become famous through it and now it had exploded in their faces — for now there was a third König to be taken into consideration. This third König was not on father's side, nor on mother's. This was the new factor which came upon both of them with a shock. Gorka was no longer the wavy haired prodigy smiling coldly and shyly from the wings before an admiring public, this was a determined and individuated being of sudden force and maturity that had emerged with the same speed as his facility to compose for full orchestra. If his teachers were shocked by his mastery of musical language, his parents were much more shocked by his mastery of himself.

Despite himself, he could not but help seeing the

conflict also from a personal point of view. That was – father is right but lacks the will to impose his authority as usual, mother is jealous and does not want me to be my own creation, I have to be hers or nothing. In all this Hitler represented the liberator who came to confirm Gorka's self-respect, self-dignity, and a talent, as much a product of German culture as of German genetics, and was that not precisely what he had done for his people, restored to them their self-respect, their dignity, won back for them their lost heritage, given them at last their own ground to stand on – to Gorka König the issue was clear. The political situation mirrored the personal one – the Munich Festival was the celebration of his freedom and of his newly found identity. The ironic element in the conflict was that to the elder Königs the third position of their son was a kind of interruption and distraction from the locked battle whose dialogue they knew so well. His decision shocked them into precipitate action.

Gorka was the calm figure in the centre of the storm. To him there was no debate – he was going to Munich as a German citizen to celebrate the new dynamism of a resurrected nation proud of its new selfhood, and to receive an honour from his and his nation's leader. More than that, he wanted his parents to know that the decision to go was not in their hands. Whether they accompanied him or not was a matter of supreme indifference to the newly emerged man who for the first time in his life saw himself as a free and self-determining human being.

The departure of Anna Sorenson to Zurich, en route for the United States, which she always presented to the world as a heroic and dangerous political act of defiance, was in itself the culmination of the three days of towering rages and incriminating quarrels that left both partners exhausted and beaten. No one tried to impede her departure, and Johann König found that he had been invited to Heidelberg on the very day of the Munich Festival to address a distinguished gathering on the theme of 'German philosophy and German morals'. Gratefully, he admitted the government had given him a way out as much to save them as him from embarrassment. Gorka König set out alone to attend the national premiere of his first symphony. He was eighteen and the world stood on the brink of war. He sensed it, but he did not understand it. It exhilarated him because he could not resist his own experience of his country's new-found vigour, and he felt within him a patriotism and pride that was not devoid of moral nobility. He knew himself as the defender of a tradition of wisdom and profundity that came from the last century and which had been cruelly and unjustly halted by the heinous punishment of the German nation by the Versailles Treaty. Now, he felt, again we are on the track of our great task, and I will play my part, and in that he knew he was not alone. He had been alone all his life, and now he felt one with his people. At that moment he was profoundly grateful to the Führer, little could he know how much that adolescent affection and inspiration would one day cost him and how bitterly he would be punished for it, but he would never deny it, never deny any part of his own reality to please anybody, if that was taken from him what was there left? Gorka König was a simple and stubborn man, but he did not know for many years what the price of being oneself cost, nor that to go against the view of the age was to be destroyed.

In retrospect Johann König realized that by not accompanying his son he enhanced the impact that the historic meeting in Munich was bound to make. With the real father figure absent the importance of the symbolic father of the nation became even more significant and took on its own definition since there was no real image to measure it against. The inevitable happened, and now that history, or as Gorka König would later say, the current version of history, has defined who the central characters are in this narrative it is difficult for the intellect to hold to any illusion of objectivity. A political judgement has become a psychiatric diagnosis – this was Johann König's phrase in his study of 'psychiatric politics' when he referred to the historical view of Adolf Hitler in current serious discourse. He did not refer to the Munich first meeting between his son and the Chancellor of Germany but there is little doubt that he had learned deeply from the results of that fateful meeting.

In this narrative of the life of Gorka König politics intrudes with the same insistence and resonance with which his life intrudes on his musical expression and, in turn, it impinges on his own philosophy and friends. However, the meeting that took place after the concert in Munich is of such importance in Gorka König's life that we can neither ignore it nor resort to a violent reaction of insult and pejorative language. Extreme positions on this subject seem still, so long afterwards, the order of the day. It is enough here to note that the reader must try to remember that the narrative involves two human beings of exceptional personality and capacities, indeed of different forms of genius, one to inspire a great nation to follow his leadership and the other to inspire that same nation to respond profoundly to his symphonic discourse.

If there was one word that could sum up their encounter after the tumultuous reception his symphony received, and that brought the Führer to his feet applauding, 'Das ist eine ewige Kunst!' then it was simply – enthusiasm! The Führer was at his most charming and animated, the attractive and cultured women around him went out of their way to take up the young composer, and the commotion that ran through the reception was that an event of cultural importance had happened and that another proof of the power and superiority of the German people had again confirmed what everybody had always known that, somehow, despite all the conflicts, military and dynastic which had for centuries so torn the people, they were the central strand of western civilization in music, philosophy and technological prowess.

During the course of the evening Gorka was invited to retire with the Führer to a private apartment. With his heart beating fast he followed the evenly paced, light, almost orientally relaxed step of the Chancellor into the salon. The door closed behind him and with a kind of panic he realized he was alone with the Führer, except for a pretty blonde girl who sat in one corner smiling encouragement at him, and while they had been introduced he had at that moment not the slightest idea who she was – he could only see before him the hypnotically alert face of Adolf Hitler, his piercing blue eyes seeming to penetrate into the depths of his being. Later he was asked in an interview to describe what he had felt emanating from his host in that meeting and he had replied, 'Kindness, and power.'

The phrase was to haunt him when the full weight of the victor's morality was to fall upon him, but that was in the future, he still lived in a time when despite the ruthless and effective power mechanism of the Nazi Party people talked openly about the charismatic and enthralling experience of meeting the German ruler.

The conversation relaxed as Gorka was made to feel at his ease and soon they were talking about Wagner, and his significance for Germany and the world. Myth and history, the future and its rich potential – a world freed from economic exploitation, freed from the curse of 'the Ring' – these were the themes that wove in and out of their conversation, or perhaps it was more of a monologue and only in retrospect seemed to contain the elements of dialogue that gave it that thrilling sense of exchange between them, but in a way this is what had happened for he had spoken first in his music and that night his Führer had replied.

One of the subjects which König later remembered from that first encounter was the concern with which the Führer had spoken about the danger of war. It was not necessary – war on the Allies. He distinctly recalled the subject coming up. The nation's army was facing Russia. The promised objective of the Third Reich was the destruction of communism, and if they did not do it what a terrible and dark destiny lay ahead for mankind. He used to tell this detail but then insist that more had been said which he – in this later time – could not tell, because it was as he put it, 'too late' and nobody would believe it. It had proved to be in his words, 'prophetic'.

As throughout his life there were incidents which happened and of which exist 'versions' which he very consciously presented to the world, that these versions contain changes in detail may be taken as a legendary aspect of his personality and may imply a character with a weak hold on the reality principle, it may well be that they were so close to him, so mixed one with another that these anecdotes emerged from him with variants as authentic signatures do, while the proof of the forged one is its identical nature when repeated. These early memories became more precious and more rare to him through the years, as the same wine changes its taste and improves yet remains the fruit of the same grape, so in the fermentation of his days these encounters with Adolf Hitler came to represent something way beyond either their historical character or their political significance, they were emblematic of forces which he perceived at work in the world and as the years unfolded their chronicle of disasters he became more and more aware that these forces had a more ominous and more devastating plan for the human race than any that was placed at the door of the leader of the German nation in the first half of the twentieth century.

Gorka König returned to Freiburg a young man, the meeting in Munich had been a rite of passage, a Wagnerian oath-taking, and a confirmation. He had left Hitler promising him another symphony, or rather, his country, as it had been put to him, expected it. He returned to find his father alone and stunned by the departure he had perhaps for some time secretly longed to see. Gorka, for his part, felt little, to his surprise it seemed as if he had turned off a flow that had once existed between him and them, and now he viewed the 'exile' as a betrayal of Hitler, himself and his father, in that romantic order. The press confirmed the view of Anna Sorenson's flight to Hollywood as treachery, and her public statements as treason itself. Johann König was accepted. Discreet and outside the mainstream of academic activity, writing and occasionally lecturing, he was seen as being part of the New Germany, and now with a son who had overnight become a national hero, he was safe, a safety then that was to become a torment later.

Gorka's eyesight prevented him going into the army and he was able to continue working on his music with an unwritten exemption from other duties in the light of his special relationship with the country's leader. In his personal life the Munich meeting had meant a commitment to a life of composition; the world, however, when it thought of Hitler in Munich thought of him with Chamberlain, Mussolini, and Daladier. When Gorka König looked back on his first visit to Berchtesgaden he did not think of the momentous events that were being shaped in the heady air of the Bavarian alpine retreat, but rather the deep personal and imaginative exchanges that had taken place between the two men in their private walks together, the contents of which he would never disclose. Whatever the content of these talks they took place in an atmosphere of urgent comings and goings, of equerries and ambassadors. These he remembers, but little grasped that in these exchanges the destinies firstly of a whole nation, Czechoslovakia, and ultimately of the whole world, were being decreed.

In 1939 as Europe again moved towards war, Gorka König was deep in his inner world of composition. His father withdrew more and more from public life but not in creative gestation, for him the outside events confirmed the deep reflections in which he had been engaged throughout his life. He came to formulate in these tense and anticipatory months before the outbreak of war his theory that men were not moved either by the mobile patternings of events or by ideologies and ideas but rather by inner drives and programming which prevent them understanding the moral mosaic in which they are and force inevitable collective action to cover up their motivation, the personal dilemma or lack.

By 1940 the Second Symphony was ready. It was performed in Berlin to a distinguished and impressive audience which received it with the same enthusiasm that they had greeted the First, but perhaps in place of the spontaneity of the Munich reaction could be noted a more serious and considered appreciation. At the same time the fact that the country was at war and yet did not feel itself to be at war gave the gala evening a festive air. The lighter and more buoyant atmosphere of the Second Symphony was taken to express the vitality and energy of the young Reich and a sign of the dynamic capacity its new generation had to confront yet again – what König later called 'the political trap of two major wars that could have been avoided'. In this period of the war, however, Gorka was living a life devoid of self-reflection. He had not yet arrived at that stage when the intellectual inheritance from his father would activate his imagination to a critical act of re-interpretation of all the basic values of the century. That he was to express his ideas not only in words but in musical symphonic discourses of vast sweep and complexity made his later views both more accessible and at the same time more impossible to access. Accessible to the sensibility and the higher mathematical function of the harmonic intellect and impossible of access to the experiencing person of the mid-century who was now totally pre-conditioned not to think about these matters, to think about any matters but categorically not about these, or one could even say this one unspeakable subject. And it was not racism, or naziism, or anything to do with the dialectic of right and left, fascist and communist in which he had grown up. This was the jump he was to make intellectually, and there is no doubt that the thoughts and struggles of his father were to play a seminal role in that inner development.

A year later Hitler ordered Gorka König to Berlin. They had a brief meeting and following that meeting the composer returned to Freiburg, closed his apartment, said goodbye to his father and crossed the border into Switzerland. He was met by officials of the German embassy and driven in a private car to Zurich. Whatever took place certainly resulted in an official welcoming party across the frontier that saw the composer securely settled in a Zurich apartment. He was to spend the rest of the war in that same house.

The war years are another of the areas of the composer's life that are shrouded in rumours and contrary versions, legends, and some downright lies which later scholarship has fortunately revealed. Of course, being the years of his youthful manhood they are obviously crucial in the formation of that creative process that resulted in the later symphonies.

3.

The first interesting observation to be made about Gorka's war years is that from the Second Symphony in 1940 until the third, written during 1945, Gorka König did not produce any work or present any before the public. Apart from his private musical studies and note-taking the only musical activity in which he participated was his enormously popular conducting in Zurich which must be counted an important part of his musical development, for a glance at the programmes reveals a systematic working through of the classical symphonic repertoire. His symphonic cycles were appreciated by the public and his conducting, rigorously inspired by Wagner's classical text on the subject – Wagner invented modern conducting, was König's dictum – was viewed as original and dynamic. His interpretation of the Tchaikovsky symphonies was considered an act of artistic discovery, like they had never been heard before, as the critics wrote, for he presented them in the now familiar manner, not as slavic essays in self-dramatization or as neurotic confessions, but rather as noble and profound meditations on these emotional themes, so that, by refusing to indulge in the romantic sweep of the music he presented the composer's command over his condition through the harmonic and structural coherence of his music.

König's life in Switzerland during the Second World War was of a special quality being as it was the vortex of calm in the storm of European war. As well as the inevitable spice of international intrigue, and the sometimes comic social dramas of life in the diplomatic world, the elite of the country lived a prosperous if isolated life and enjoyed their peaceful existence as well as the titillation of war news that filtered across the borders. Among the friends that became familiar at Gorka's residence was a group of expatriate Yugoslavian diplomats from the exiled royal entourage who had taken refuge in Switzerland. They in turn moved among the small group of exiles from the various earthquakes that had shaken the political power structure of Europe. Their friends were White Russians, an exotic and socially dubious crew, whose star was a Romanoff princess of delicious social grace. Their passion for music took them into the orbit of König who was charmed by their style and their formality and passion for political discourse. It was of a kind he had not heard before and while the ideas were without doubt predictable, for these people were as much historical products as the Allied soldiers or the intellectuals who were busy re-defining the cause of war to be read as a defence of western civilization to prepare Europe to forget that the pretext had been the liberation of Poland, nevertheless the views of the group involved elements of thinking that were the unique province of a certain political elite and were not that of the press and the so-called educated class.

His first meeting with the Yugoslavians had been at a private dinner party. He found himself next to Borjas Puric, then acting Prime Minister for the exiled King, although his true rank had been Premier Ambassadeur in Paris. He was a well built man of heavy good looks and a quality of charm that made him very popular. When he had been Consul in Los Angeles Valentino used to visit him secretly in order to read his poetry to him. He was a man of confidences, personal and political. Feeling a little uneasy beside the mature and distinguished diplomat König thought he might be disapproved of as having a personal link with Adolf Hitler. To his astonishment Puric began to make an appraisal of the war in Europe which did not contain in it any condemnation of Germany. Carefully he asked the Yugoslavian if he did not feel hatred for the people that had over-run his country. Puric looked at him in amazement as if he were stupid, as if somehow he had failed to understand his every word.

'But my dear sir! Don't you understand what is happening? Is it not clear to you? Do you never look at the maps? You study the score before you conduct. Our score is the map of Europe and its changes. What do you think is happening?'

Gorka pointed out that he had asked him twice, could he be so kind as to tell him, since, apparently he did not know. Puric, with all his most effective charm calmed the young maestro and launched into the first of what was to be one of many pointed and brief discourses on the history of the century and the reason that he found himself drawn into their delightful and rootless circles.

'The whole world has been told that the cause of the war in 1914 was the assassination of the Arch-Duke Ferdinand and his wife. Please permit us the right to speak on what concerns our national destiny. As Serbs we are entitled to a voice in the matter. We certainly wanted our freedom. Who killed the unfortunate little Hapsburg? 'The Black Hand'? A secret society! Was it ours? Did we send swarms of secret societies all over Europe? Did the so-called Young Turks do the same in Turkey, and then the secret societies in Russia, and so on? My dear sir – it simply was not us. Now here is an interesting thing. If we then try to talk about conspiracy – if we then put forward our evidence we are told we are crazy. But everybody knows these organizations existed, were connected to each other, used the same political language and methods and proposed the same legendary programme of national liberations. We were tricked in 1914. So was Germany. Do you really think the Kaiser wanted that stupid war? His biography will be rewritten until in the end you believe he was some kind of a monster or a fool when we all know he was just a simple fellow caught in matters way beyond his comprehension. And today – I tell you this, and do not forget that German troops occupy our land and German planes have bombed our capital – your Führer has been duped. And he will lose. I know he did not want the war, he had another programme – my opinion of that is another matter – but in his Reichstag speech he openly offered peace and it was refused. Wait and see, my friend. Wait and see. Communism must be rescued. It is part of a coherent plan. Why? You see, this war will end 'politics' and 'economics' – role up the map of Europe, it will not be needed and so on. You do not understand? I am ancien régime? No! I am the radical!'

König was intrigued but unconvinced. Yet the mixture of power politics and poetry in the conversation delighted him as if to awaken him those memories of late summer evenings in his childhood when his parents and their circle of fascinating friends had talked and talked about just such things in that heady atmosphere of good Havana and French scent. From this one-sided conversation began his entry into Puric's circle and from that meeting with a woman who was to captivate him and hold him enthralled during the period he would later refer to as his 'prison years in Switzerland'.

The war years were indeed a prison for him, cutting him off from the mainstream of the time, full-scale and barbaric war with 'unconditional surrender' as its final condition. To those who believed the dominant propaganda, that meant to be finished once and for all with the risk of German militarism as a threat to 'western civilisation', though how this could be conceived of without the German genius which was its central dynamism was never explained. To the small circle around König it meant that the coherent and step-by-step conquest of Europe could move to its next phase by the elimination of the one force that could impede its growth, and that what they had done half-heartedly in the Versailles Treaty with an ending to the war that guaranteed its recommencement, this time they would do definitively and move onto the next part of the Plan – though what that plan was they had not at that stage discussed with him. While constantly denying they were conspiracy-theorists, with the same constancy they insisted that to talk of this subject was the most dangerous thing in the world. While they withheld from him the inner elements of their world-view they were generous in sweeping him into the social swirl of the Slav expatriate community and he was pleased that his Germanness did not exclude him from their circle. While other social circles talked of nothing but the war, he was aware that to these cultured and intellectually sophisticated people there existed a view of life that did not contain this partisan division of life into 'us and them' which so informed everybody else, a trait he was to be more aware of after the war than during it. It was in this somewhat rare and rarefied group that he met the young woman around whom his war years in Switzerland were to circle in a hopeless and tangled love affair he was never to forget, or get out of his system.

Milena was not beautiful, yet those who knew her would swear she was, some photographs of her suggest she was, but she really was, and in no small measure, alluring. The eyes were pure Slav, slightly slanted, two gleaming jetstones, constantly making their appearance from behind sweeping lashes on a head that never looked straight but always from a tilted angle of mockery or invitation or approval. She used her hands with affected grace, tilting back the small finger in an almost vulgar manner, except in her it suggested Marie Antoinette shielding her eyes from the light in the Temple prison, for she seemed incapable of vulgarity, in her, every gesture or phrase was transformed into a high theatrical and sexual style. In fact she was often shockingly vulgar in her speech by way of deliberate offence but she transformed it into some kind of social challenge as if to say that is what you deserve or that is the only language you understand, if angry, and, isn't this naughty, if pleased. Her black hair cut above the shoulder was brushed out like a tennis player's, loose and dishevelled framing the marvellous eyes and accentuating the Slav cheekbones. She was small. One day she would be fat, but no man could look at her and think such a thing. Well, some could for there were two reactions to her among men, one that she was a crazy whore and the other that she was an irresistibly attractive aristocrat. Of course, she was both. And it was in the crisis of his youthful years that Gorka König, captivated, had to swing from the latter view, and then, unbearably, and broken-hearted, to the former. The pictures of them together are moving in their romantic perfection. They seem so right together, she seems so much the kind of woman you want a great composer to have by his side, and this was part of the drama for them – what other people wanted them to be. That they should be together was delightful for other people. It was perfect for the decor of social life, and for the romantic imagination. That they should part was unthinkable but the reason why they should not was that it offended this same projected fantasy that others had of them as the ideal couple. It had of course all those same elements of disaster that precipitated the break-up of the König-Sorenson marriage, but at that time and at his age Gorka König saw nothing of that, he lived only through 'total intoxication with you and desolation without'. They played games like children, and they were in many ways orphans of the storm, cast into the game of being adult in a fragmented society with the parents elsewhere, somewhat distracted, because the whole world they had known was blowing up in their faces. 'Wars are for adults, the Führer said to me. And I understood. Children hated them,' König wrote to Milena. She wrote back long reams of cultured and childish insights quoting from Romain Rolland, exalting the 'darling child' Mozart, and 'my beloved B.' projecting the perfect Romantic image of the male, Lord Byron, out beyond any real male, so it was clear that no man could ever make her happy, thus in the end she would have to retreat into her dream. He saw none of this, he saw a woman come so close to him that they almost merged, more brother and sister than lovers, their friends said, yet everyone saw the bond, the fated bond that is sealed between two people so that once it exists no one can come between and once they are apart no one can ever get near. When she went with other men, they came seeking him out, talking to him of her, causing him anguish, while they, in their own desperation, jealous, begged him to decode her for them. But when he talked of her, they fled back in total confusion, knowing they could not know any intimacy like that intimacy, that oneness. He spoiled other men for her by his continued existence, and she spoiled herself for him to scar forever his continued existence.

Together they illuminated any gathering they attended. Apart they were the source of endless utterly satisfying gossip and malice. Their being together, on and off, over the war years was a superb theatrical event, like two great actors reciting verse on an empty stage, or, in her language, a Verdi duet, for it excluded everybody else so completely, that in the end others were glad to see it play itself out, a necessary, diverting, but nevertheless excessive spectacle. Unfortunately, by the time the war ended and she left for England it was clear to everyone, even poor Gorka, that his Milena had gradually, and with an actress's genius, concealed until the very last that she had subtly, glass by glass, party by party, and bar by bar, turned into a classical alcoholic, with a bottle of spirits carefully wrapped in brown paper tucked, on every occasion, into her handbag, which in turn grew larger to accommodate those things which she, more and more, compulsively had to carry about with her, as she slid gently into a world of her own.

It was to be the end of the war that brought Gorka

König out of his personal and insular world and his neurotic obsession with a hopeless love affair already dead into a world of painful and urgent new politics. In an atmosphere of general rejoicing he seemed once again to find himself alone. While others celebrated an end to hostilities and spoke grandly about a victory for western civilization over barbarism, König seemed immediately aware that far from having left a dark age mankind was now entering one. With four million dead German combatants and one million tons of bombs dropped on its cities, with the terrible loss of life this had caused in the civilian population, the nation had also been shattered in morale by a second massive military defeat in the same century. On top of all this tragic suffering, Gorka knew all too well that a further and more cutting edge of punishment awaited the German people, one that would cut to the heart of its life-force and spiritual being. He knew, there and then, that with every year as the renewed force of the enemy grew stronger, Germany would pay a terrible price for – for what he could no longer speak about because nobody would even be able to listen. He wrote:

> 'I saw in 1945 that the very issues which had been the vital issues of the century would now be buried in a passionate re-appraisal of values which would prevent people from examining

the crucial theme that I had learned about in the strange empty war years where I was able to view the whole charade by which what had been a calculated scheme to destroy civilization was turned into a crusade to save it. How many years would it take before even the most remote chance of objectivity might dawn? How long before the dissenting voice would not be silenced or drowned by cries of insane, insane?'

While people danced in the streets of the capitals of Europe König shut his door and began his Third Symphony and gave it the name of 'The Dark Night'. He worked, feverishly determined to finish it and at the same time desperate to make contact with his father having learned that he was still alive. Contact by telephone was impossible and he decided that as soon as the work was completed he would simply set out to reach Freiburg.

In 1945 the war began for Gorka König. His first shock was when he presented the news of the symphony's completion to his colleagues in Zurich. To his amazement he found that there was an atmosphere of extreme hostility, as if his former friends seemed afraid to associate themselves with him for fear of some contamination or rejection similar to what now was clearly waiting for the composer. Not slowly, but brutally and crudely it was borne in on him that he was to be punished – he was to be rejected – he was to be branded as a Nazi. And as he stood, frozen by the utterly unexpected insult of having a distinguished musician spit in his face as he tried to enter the cafe for his usual morning gathering of friends, König lifted his hand to wipe his face and was heard to exclaim, 'Oh my God – what will they do to Father?' When he arrived at his apartment he locked the door as if he expected a mob to besiege him. He sat down in the salon and stared straight ahead unable to move or think, paralysed as the situation dawned on him. He has written and spoken of these days often, for the double impact of having his music rejected and his father imperilled at the same time not only presented him with a conflict of loyalties, one to his art the other to his family, but flung him cruelly and unprepared in front of a hostile world without any protection from his reputation or his name.

He was already packed and ready to leave for Germany when he received word from Freiburg that his father had sent a message to him telling him it would not be safe for him to return to his country at this time. 'At this time' – the irony did not escape him. The war was over and his father needed him but he could not go to him for, although he had spent almost all the war years in neutral Switzerland, 'at this time' he was a suspect. As one newspaper was to write about him, 'Do we want to listen to the music of this man who has walked and talked with the Devil?'

The sudden crisis into which he was catapulted brought out a new and incisive element in his character. He made judicious contacts in Geneva and began to put together a picture of how things were in occupied Germany. Freiburg was under French occupation. He soon realized that the plight of his country was much worse than in 1918, for if the French in a bitter replay of history wanted the Saar, this time, Communist Russia had one half of the nation. Bitterly, he enquired, 'And have they liberated Poland from the Dictator?'

Piece by piece he reconstructed the last days of the Reich as best he could. He learned that Hitler's ultimate political act had been the dismissal of Himmler and Goering, and the appointment of Grand Admiral Dönitz. He heard the first tales of revenge and punishment by the victors, but he knew that the real dangers lay ahead when the dust of war had cleared. He hung on for several weeks while his friends tried to dissuade him from making the journey, while he, for his part, sought a way to reach the nearby, but so inaccessible, city where his father lived. Finally, convinced that his presence was necessary to the safety of his father he decided to take the risk and cross the border. As he waited for a friend, a Swiss diplomat who had insisted on driving with him, another car drew up in front of the apartment. A letter was delivered to him as he stood on the pavement outside his house. He opened it and read. The letter dropped out of his hands and he walked down the icy street, his face ashen, his steps faltering. Just then the other car arrived. His friend followed him down the slippery street and put an arm around him. König turned to face him, shocked. 'Dr Webern. They've killed him. In the doorway of his house – they shot him. The Americans have shot him.' They were the first words that he said to his father when he embraced him in Freiburg. His education had begun.

In a sense König's arrival in Germany in 1945 obliged him to catch up with the war, and with the whole story of what had happened to his country not only during those five years but also the whole saga of the post-Weimar years. He realized that his youth and his personal regard for the Führer had also in some way isolated him from taking in the politics of his epoch so that now, with his country in ruins about him, he had to sit down with a father estranged from him by time and by prejudice and beg him to tell him what had happened in the years that were his life. He returned to Freiburg to be shocked both by the physical condition of his father who was seriously undernourished and by his psychic energy which was low and melancholy. He stared long and bleakly at his son and confessed at last to him: 'For the same reasons that I could not in the end support Hitler, now, I cannot support this charade of moral superiority that is being paraded before the German people. We –' he said it meaning the Germans, and Gorka immediately understood – 'we are at the same time being asked to be profoundly ashamed of ourselves as if we had betrayed our humanity, and were a form of ultimate disgrace to the species, and also behave as if the Americans and their cohorts had finally liberated us from a nightmare, or brought us round from some mass hallucination in which the whole people inexplicably plunged themselves for a decade. Were we mad for ten years? Were we obsessed Satans for ten years? Were we brutalized victims of a regime we never really wanted? Were we stupid, dupes of history? Gorka, this that is happening now is worse than any physical horror, this is the deliberate destruction of the German heritage and German spirit. Wait and see – in a year or so you will be ashamed to say you love Wagner. The Meistersingers will be an obscenity which to admire will be an unspeakable ideological crime. You will not be able to read Nietzsche, conduct Wagner or Strauss, and I doubt if it will even be safe for you to express a taste for vegetarian food!' He tried a wry smile but Gorka saw his father for the first time near to tears. He looked up at his son, his face open in anguish, unconcealed, 'I – I cannot even bring myself to speak about what they are going to do about our philosophy...' It was in that meeting, Gorka later confirmed, that he began to love his father for the first time.

They talked through the night, 'for twenty-four hours', Gorka later said. It was as if they had never talked before – never once entered a realm outside the closed tense family dramas that far from binding them together, had over these years held them apart – and for the first time they together looked at the age they lived in with dispassion and detachment and with a vision for the future and at the same time coldly taking into account the new irrationalism that was being paraded before the world as the ultimate and irreducible foundation of human justice and civilization. Gorka explained as best he could the concepts of Puric and his compatriots, trying to sift from the ideas those elements which he felt forced to reject in as much as they supported the monarchist past, while aware that precisely because they had been in the places of high power they had seen for that brief space of time the naked mechanisms of a complex and yet straightforward scheme for the re-designing of the world system in the last quarter of the twentieth century. Johann realized in these exchanges in a way much more profoundly than he had known in his philosophical discourse that he had not been wrong, had not made a mistake, and that the utterly vital historical core of western civilization risked being obliterated and a cynical sham put in its place, rhetorically declaring itself for human rights and justice and democracy and all the high linguistic decoration of morality while in itself it would be an empty and vicious decadence with no intellectual future, rats would sport among the ruins, but where once there had been a noble aspiration there would remain only a worthless monetary exchange.

The very next day both Johann and Gorka König were arrested. They were separated, as if they had been witness to a crime and had to be kept apart in case they tried to make their evidence corroborative. Johann König, existential philosopher, found himself in front of his inquisitor, an American soldier whose peacetime occupation had been that of a Hollywood script-writer. His response, which he repeated again and again, 'The questions you ask will give you the answers you desire,' enraged his captors. He did not deny that he had joined the Nazi Party. Over six million Germans had belonged to National Socialist organizations. Yes.

And they would all be investigated. 'The cause of the war has been altered.' The inability of his inquisitor to understand his answers let alone his philosophical opinions which were, though utterly incomprehensible, there and then defined as dangerous and subversive to the human spirit, made the interrogations as much a personal encounter between ignorance and prejudice as those almost identical encounters to be found in ancient Chinese historical chronicles where the bloody force of the victors wiped out the wisdom of the defeated. He saw it for what it was, a mockery of everything that they pretended to hold sacred in that mythical realm 'international law' – 'international law has been invented to create a nation that does not adhere to the same terms of nationhood as every other nation and it will bring about the downfall of your world' – for now a hybrid international kangaroo court was putting on trial the German people for its own conduct of its own affairs within its sovereign boundaries during the years in which it was not at war with its enemies as well as in the war years themselves. They were not interested in his 'case', only his role, his commitment to the policies of the Nazi Party and so on, they interrogated him again and again, mixing political and social events, asking him his views, so that his mind was on trial at one minute and his actions the next. Yes, he had delivered an address at Heidelberg University at the invitation of the Government. Yes, he stood by its contents in substance. No, he did not align himself with the doctrines and actions of Himmler. He doubted if Himmler could align himself with his existential philosophy, and besides had not the Führer dismissed Himmler from office before they had taken him into custody? He did not appear to his inquisitors to be repentant or express those necessary emotions of shock and shame that they demanded. Recalcitrant, said one judge; out of touch noted another more benignly. Judgment was passed forbidding him to hold any post or lecture at any university or officially registered institution of learning throughout Germany, any publication would first have to be submitted to a court or other body later appointed.

Gorka's investigation was even stranger. Bonded to an inescapable fascination for the person of the Führer and all personal information about him, his captors sometimes appeared to be more fanatical admirers and lovers of the late Chancellor than to be his victorious and hating enemies. It seemed to Gorka König at times that they were jealous rather than horrified by the friendship which he stubbornly refused to deny. What could it mean to them? What could they see? He saw that they had been indoctrinated over the years with an extraordinarily naive and often childish view not only of Adolf Hitler but the German people. The Germans had been enemies to them for five years and for a lifetime of propaganda and to their parents also for another lifetime. While the interrogators who had tested his father had stumbled about in a high syntax of philosophical discourse looking for overt political confessions, those who examined Gorka tried to find allusions and loyalties in phrases and style of music between himself and Wagner, an affinity inescapable by his homage in the title of his First Symphony but unrecognizable in style except for the famous opening and closing bars which in 1945 were taken to imply a naked admission of adherence to Nazi doctrines real and imagined. He could not maintain the detachment of his father, for he was not so ill and his youthful vigour inspired by his newly emerging political understanding made him seethe with rage at the arrogance and duplicity of the whole procedure, with its lawyers and experts all pretending to some kind of higher justice. 'And is the man who killed Anton von Webern a murderer or a soldier and a hero?' They did not know who Anton von Webern was and informed him that he and not this Webern person was the subject of the investigation. In the end they released him under restrictive rulings similar to those to which they had submitted his father. Basically he was sentenced to remain a private person. Gorka returned to his father's house with the exclamation, 'I will not become a Nazi now, just to please them, when I never did so for the Führer, and he never asked me to!' When interviewed by a reasonably sympathetic musical journal from France about his views on these burning post-war obsessions he replied: 'These are not the issues!' Asked what the issues were he shrugged and said, 'To raise the issues we may have to wait fifty, a hundred years. Please do not ask me now.'

Gorka at that time simply did not see how he could present his case without being branded as a barbarian, the pejorative language had so brilliantly been blended with the vocabulary of humanism and civilization, as if the military victory of those avaricious allies bound together for the most ruthless of materialist goals allowed them to claim with mystic fervour they were the protectors of all human values and culture, that any dissenting voice was inescapably defined as criminal. All justice, for the first time in world history claimed to be on the side of the victors on a global scale – what a vast crime must be about to be committed, was Gorka's response. And, more than that, what a crime they had committed already by unleashing upon the world the weapons of ultimate destruction. In the ensuing years he was to watch with his incredulity stretched to the limits as the world was ordered to take the creators of the nuclear weapon as heroes and great men. Not a year went by without his original perception of the truth of his century being confirmed by new events, but that is a theme beyond the scope of this biographical summary, what is important to understand is that in 1945 he did not consider himself in possession of those facts which he later claimed justified totally his rejection of the dominant monetarist regime which he realized at last held the world in its thrall.

The result of the so-called de-nazification trials convinced Gorka König that he should remain in his country. 'We must sit out the years of the mediocratic power system,' his father had counselled to him, insisting that sooner or later the wheel would turn. Neither of them was prepared for the deep depressive gloom in which the victors plunged Europe as they plotted to set up their new postpolitical world. The so-called Cold War plunged Europe into a darkness and moral vacuum whose depths could not be measured. All the joy of life had been sucked away, all the energy and drive, all the celebration of existence, a puritanism that mitigated against life itself and not just pleasure turned Europe into a dismal prison run by faceless men in grey suits, heavy long overcoats and brimmed hats. The Russian was indistinguishable from the American, the capitalist from the communist. In all of it only one force could be felt, the natural and vital force of the German people, heroically, and alas blindly, working to rehabilitate yet again their shattered and this time divided homeland. It was against this background that Gorka became his father's philosophy student.

4.

The official branding of the Königs as Nazi sympathizers by their more liberal friends not only set them apart from the awakening life of post-war Europe but also brought father and son closer together. Gorka had his unformed but vibrant political views to impart and his father found that for the first time he was able to go directly from his philosophical foundations to direct demonstration and application in the ruined world that surrounded them. Gorka's view of a world in which the whole power structure operated along a totally different set of integers from that propounded and taught in public dialogue was not backed up by sufficient evidence and not made comprehensible through his lack of any capacity for formal thinking. What he could say musically he could not express in the realm of concepts, while his father extended himself, and opened himself up to being an existential thinker in the true sense of applying his inner reality to impact on the world outside. Gorka experienced a frustration that combined his inability to say what he meant with a resentment that he was not accepted by society after a lifetime of being the world's darling. It was in this state of intense loneliness and bitterness that he met Frieda Ludendorff. She was a writer and a psychiatrist, popular, radical and to Gorka König highly desirable. She was socially vivacious and in private pensive and attentive. She knew how to pay total attention so that when another spoke it was as if there was nothing more important than their words, nothing more necessary than a reply worthy of the compliment of that confidence. It was not love at first sight, it was intimacy at first sight.

What Frieda Ludendorff brought to the Königs was an opening into the world of psychiatric thinking without the, to them, antiscientific and determinist view of Freud, 'the Viennese novelist' as Johann König called him. She helped Johann to think in psychiatric terms in a manner which widened and physicalized his whole methodology and it was in conversation with her that he first put forward his dialectic of what he named 'psychiatric politics' which was to play such a key role in his 'The Limits of Consciousness and the Limits of Power'.

To Gorka König Frieda brought recognition with intimacy which for him more than replaced the public recognition in which he used to bask. Her understanding of his gifts, her encouragement of his new desire to enter the realms of politics and philosophy expanded and deepened his intellectual character, and what was most valuable to him as a man was that he was able to see that this gift came from her and not from his own natural talent. It was she who showed him that he could be a composer with a philosophy and a political viewpoint and that each would illuminate and explain the other.

By 1946 they were married and the König circle became again one of the most interesting and desirable circles to enter in Europe. Only this time it was private, small and exclusive, where before it had been loose and large and in the deliberate glare of public attention. With the balance of time tilting to the new generation, 'the Königs' were now a distinguished composer and his clever psychiatrist wife, they were the couple, the third was no longer a precocious child genius but an erudite, withdrawn and melancholy man of great knowledge and sweetness who did not wish to impose his view on anyone, for he preferred to leave the dialectic to his son and daughter-in-law. Slowly, with the years, he was taking on, unaware, the role of the rejected philosopher, Oedipus at Colonus, a man reconciled to destiny in a world which scarcely seemed to be aware of its own existence, so lacking in self-consciousness did it seem to him. He was interviewed by a weekly and asked for his view of the post-war world. He refused, saying he did not have a view of it. They asked him to advise a philosophy for the young post-war German. He told them that he recommended they become interrogative anti-Cartesians, when they asked him to explain he merely said: 'I am – therefore should I not think?' The interview was not published.

Frieda brought Gorka to life. She gave him confidence and taught him to enjoy himself, without any of his mother's frivolity yet with enormous social enthusiasm she opened up to him the world of society, teaching him to be tolerant of different kinds of people, people who were not 'like' them yet interesting. She taught him how to read people so that basically he could not make a mistake. She cautioned him: 'You'll never misjudge a person now, unless, that is, you want to go to bed with them.' To Gorka the discovery of the self was as much of a surprise as the world of music had been. 'They are the same,' Frieda used to tell him, 'the notation is limited but the expression is endless.' They enjoyed each other, they quoted each other. She questioned him, drove him on, confirmed his quest. With her he explained for the first time his views on women that he had learned from Wagner and she seemed to embody in a most intellectual way that view of the woman completing the man, saving him. 'Christianity is the denial of woman as having a unique and utterly vital role. They make holy motherhood, that does not even need the man and is not the result of sensual delight, as the meaning of woman. I see now,' she wrote to him, 'how in Wagner woman is the key to man.'

He would confide in her the Wagner conversations he had had walking in the Bavarian snows with the Führer and how he had reminded him that Wagner was writing a piece on the role of women in the new society at the time of his death in the Palazzo in Venice. 'Women are not supposed to like Wagner, they are supposed to disapprove of him. We are supposed to love Mozart and feel morally superior. Ah – Mozart! We'd better save that one up for our reunion next week.' When apart their conversation continued in talkative letters which they wrote almost daily. Many are filled with banalities as one would expect, and why not, but there flashes through them at times the key light of an inspiration that they both seemed to share, and their passion to comprehend the movements of their times and the direction in which the world was heading make them still fascinating reading.

By 1950 Gorka had completed the Fourth Symphony without ever having heard the Third. It was Frieda with her social contacts and popularity that began to open up again to the composer of ill-repute the world of music, and its politics and tactics. She picked a careful way among the various factions, making friends across a wide political spectrum, enlisting the so-called liberals, challenging them that König should not be punished musically for his political youth. They were still living in a musically censored society. Bayreuth had survived by a miracle of sympathetic forces coming together just in time to save it, but it was still preferable that one's musical taste should be free of ideological crime.

König refused to allow the Fourth to be performed until he had heard the Third. Its title and its date of composition somehow guaranteed bad reception but König stubbornly refused. Frieda went ahead with her lobbying until at last she was able to arrange a performance of the Third in Stuttgart. It was a drab affair in a dark age and the deep tragic nature of the work seemed to assure that the evening would be one of apocalyptic gloom. The hall was packed. The orchestra was excellent and when Gorka König took the podium, to his astonishment, he was greeted with a wave of warm, respectful and appreciative applause. The hush that settled on the audience before the first sombre chord of the opening movement turned to an intense and emotional feeling of collective recognition of the musical expression. Gorka König seemed to be telling his people that what they had felt in their hearts had not been an illusion. They, in the music, with him, looked back on greatness, looked unflinchingly on chaos, and at the end looked into the total darkness with hope. It had happened again. The audience were on their feet, screaming and shouting and waving, and calling him back, and back again. They would not let him go and the lights were put on and he just stood there and a hush fell on the concert hall. He looked at them with tears in his eyes. 'I have no encore for you tonight. If I had it would be that noble melody – by Haydn.' From somewhere in the back of the hall it began until they were all singing it together, their national anthem. Gorka's triumph was complete. They had understood.

Now, when everybody has the same version of history and entertains not the slightest doubt as to its veracity it is difficult even to grasp how ambiguous feelings still were about the outcome of the war in 1950. The division of Berlin followed by the shameful Potsdam Agreement which seemed to be a determined attempt to destroy the historical Germany with even more ferocity than the Versailles Treaty had left a bitter taste in the mouth of the defeated nation. Again the punitive reparations, again the dismantling of the German industrial nexus, these combined with the ruthless relocation of millions of eastern Germans and the utterly cynical Nuremberg Trials with all their resultant implications for world justice as well as for the way in which Germans would view their own role in the war had not left the whole country docile and servile, begging forgiveness from humanity. There were, even in that climate of witch-hunting and guilt by ideological association, many influential people who could not accept what was being done, in the name of some superior justice, to the German nation. Gorka König's Third Symphony spoke with profundity to a people who stood before the world accused of being devoid of moral character. The confirmation of their own nobility and courage that so moved audiences when they first heard the symphony and the inevitable patriotic outburst that had terminated the first performance guaranteed a new reputation and a new notoriety to its composer.

The immediate result was that Gorka had offers from more than one city begging the honour of presenting the premiere of his Fourth. At the same time he became a target in the new and sophisticated ideological soft war that was being waged to reshape the thinking of an entire culture. A certain moral view was being set up in the press and in a few years also on television which was to ensure only one view of war and peace, only one concept of economics, only one dialectic of left and right. Anyone who tried to move against that stream would find himself defined as implicitly psychotic or fanatical but, most especially, against humanity. In a way it was König's success with his Third and the equally rapturous reception that greeted his Fourth, that set him down to be a target for the mass media, for the politicians who wanted to demonstrate their loyalty to the new ideology, and a whipping boy for those who saw themselves as the defenders of the new society.

Gorka König would not define himself as a Nazi, or a fascist, as the popular term had become. He was aware that the issue, that vital issue which he wanted to grasp, clarify and declare had not yet come into his intellectual life in such a way that he felt prepared to speak up about it to the world. He was still searching, enquiring, and learning. What he learned shocked him and what he knew depressed him for he could not see any way of breaking the brilliant dialectical barrier against a contrary view without being branded as the very thing he categorically rejected. He also knew that in his viewpoint lay the only future of mankind, and the reason for this was that he already grasped that in his view lay the necessary continuity in western civilization that had been brutally interrupted by a global war.

Whether he liked it or not he became a focus for dissident opinion. Some of it appalled him, he did not want to be taken up as the leader of a romantic return to the political struggles of his youth. That era was past and irrecoverable. There were new problems and new things were happening, new schemes were being hatched but he had not found the methodology that allowed him to understand them, and he was determined to avoid the same prejudicial scenario of the good and the bad used by the enemy. So it was with some trepidation that he agreed to his wife's suggestion that they go to the United States not only to visit the American poet, Ezra Pound, but throw in their weight with those other writers and artists struggling for his release. When Frieda explained what was at issue as she understood it he had no doubts any more and knew he had to go. The poet accused of being a fascist and a traitor but who heroically went on protesting he was a patriot and that the issue was the criminal nature of the monetary system not his view of human nature, was a man close to his own intellect. The details themselves outraged him as he learned of Pound's arrest by American troops in 1945, and how he had been imprisoned in an animal cage in the open air for a period of months through the bitter winter, and how, in that intolerable imprisonment, he had composed The Pisan Cantos, an undoubted masterpiece of the English language and a great statement of human nobility. In the same prison camp he had translated the Analects of Confucius, and Sophocles. Brought back to the United States a captive, a show trial had been set up to try him as a traitor and in that trial equate treason to the USA with fascism. When they realized that Pound, despite the all but unbearable trauma of his confinement, had decided to defend himself, a solution had to be found. In 1941 he had returned to America to persuade Roosevelt not to enter the war, but the idea that an American President should take counsel from a poet, let alone a poetic genius, was considered eccentric, and, bitterly unhappy, Pound had returned to Europe. If at this juncture he did put before the people what the true issue of the century had been, that it was not the hysterical issue of bestiality versus civilization but something much more real and actual involving human greed and passion on a recognizable historical stage, if he was allowed to demythologize, to declare to the world that they were victims of an emotional deception and a political trick, the process, that process which had just been embarked upon and whose pattern was not yet clear to König, would be in jeopardy. Pound was declared 'insane and mentally unfit for trial'. It was an overt victory for the psychiatrists in their role as political guardians of the new morality. A man said he was fit to defend himself, and that became part of the evidence of his insanity. He did not stand a chance. Sedated, and exhausted, on trial before he had time to recuperate from the gruelling military transportation that had brought him into the country, he was bustled off to a mental hospital in Washington, DC.

'They destroyed Webern,' wrote König to his father, 'it is clear that they also want to destroy Pound. I pray God every day for your safety.' The Königs arrived in New York in the early 1950s to a frosty press reception. Despite their desire to keep their visit private somehow it had been publicized and the couple found themselves the target of a vicious and highly imaginative press. As a result of this unpleasant publicity König found himself, quite unpreparedly, flung into another encounter with his mother. Strangest of all, this time it was Anna Sorel, as she had become, who came to defend him from a hostile regime. Having arrived on the eve of the European war as a political exile, and having made full use of her role as political heroine, she had been greeted ecstatically not only by the press but by an eager Hollywood only too glad to take up a European anti-Nazi and launch her on the world as a one-woman publicity programme representing the higher human values of the West against German barbarism. To that end she was immediately launched on the American public as a screen goddess. They bleached her hair, they plucked her eyebrows, they scooped out some flesh to highlight her cheekbones, they broke her voice, and let loose upon the world the new Anna Sorel. She married her producer, and became famous as the prostitute with the heart of gold, in Belle Epoque Paris, in a gold mining saloon on the Yukon, in earthquake-torn San Francisco. She sang in her awful voice, projecting an ironic sexuality full of innuendo and desire. The greater they said she was, the more vulgar and worthless were the vehicles that elevated her to stardom. Drunken geniuses were hired to write her scripts, only to be fired and replaced by hacks. In a career of utter vulgarity and total popularity no one knew any longer what was fantasy and what was reality, what they did know was that Anna Sorel made money. Anna Sorenson's guilt and her genuine affection for her son forced her into the quixotic role of riding East to save him from the vicious press attacks. The studio were horrified, and ran after her. They could not stop it, so they decided on a compromise. They concocted their story – the fascist composer had been saved by his brilliant psychiatrist wife and the wise counselling of his forgiving mother. His reunion with his mother was his espousal of democratic values. In the shoot-out, the goodies had won! In a suite at the Waldorf, with its hideous pseudo-European evocation of an epoch that had never existed except in some decorator's imagination, the three Königs sat together staring at each other in total silence. They had nothing to say to each other, some force outside them had temporarily won, and Gorka and Frieda knew as they had not known in Europe that the threat was real, that the war was on, and that the world was being bought.

The Pound faction were a mixed bag, firstly there were the loyal friends, then the genuine supporters of his cause, outraged by the shame that America's greatest poet had to be incarcerated among the mad, after them came a smaller and more interesting group, their concern was anti-psychiatry, and they viewed it as even more sinister that these pseudo-scientists could serve a political end in the name of some false expertise about the self, and lastly there were the pro-fascist activists who saw in Pound not only a hero but a martyr. The Königs did not know Pound but they understood the issues. Frieda was involved both in the human issue and in the psychiatric issue and she was convinced that what was needed was a historical study of what the effects and goals of psychiatry were politically, and that its method needed a critical examination not in clinical terms but in ideological ones. Gorka openly identified the punishment of Pound with the isolation and silencing of his father. Also it implied more clues to the subject that intrigued him most – the hidden causes of the war and the key to the century. In meeting Pound he had a sense of having arrived at a fountain of knowledge and that in drinking from the master's wisdom the secrets of his time would be unlocked to him. In no way was the meeting a disappointment.

Pound sat by the window staring out at some distant object that Gorka instinctively knew did not exist. A small group stood around the room making it seem crowded. They spoke in quiet but relaxed voices, smiling, touching, confirming some common bond. The poet seemed like a sombre statue of himself, so still and self-absorbed did he appear. A handsome woman in her sixties lent down and whispered to him. He turned and looked across the room at Gorka with his alert, piercing eyes. He began to hum softly and nodded, smiling. It was the theme of the Andante of his First Symphony. The two men moved towards each other, it was like old friends uniting after a long absence and they silently embraced. Pound led König back to the window and sat him down beside him. The others seemed hushed as if straining for some word of significance to report back to waiting allies, but they could hear nothing of what transpired.

Gorka was excited, moved and excited, for the poet's brilliant intellect impressed itself on him immediately – the 'madman' who could translate Sophocles and Confucius, and in his cage prison forgive his enemies, accept. Pound talked in rapid bursts, in a coherent but shortened telex English like some of his didactic writing. In that meeting it was as if all the years of intellectual confusion and contradiction were suddenly clarified as a powerful lens in one twist turns an abstract form into a clear landscape. Later Gorka confessed that he missed much for the allusions were too rapid, the images too vivid, but all the time Pound was explaining, teaching, encouraging.

König felt like a lover, who regrets not having met the beloved earlier to have shared this place and that person. He wanted the Purics here now to tell of their experience, his father to expound his own ideas. He felt ignorant and regretted that he had not read up his economics for much of what Pound said flew past him, but the ideas were dynamic and virile and radical. The gaps, the sudden lapses into instant fatigue, the renewed energy, all served to make the encounter more powerful, and the impact deeper.

'It seemed also that everything was discussed. All culture, every aspect of it, and history and civilization, and theories and concepts, and names and movements. I was in the presence of a Universal Man, who somehow had taken in the highlights and darknesses of his age with a clear understanding. He was so damned intelligent – how they must envy him, his enemies. He knows – I tell you he knows the whole story – it is a miracle he is alive. Now that I have sat with him, how cheap the epithets and adjectives with which they think they can dismiss this giant of poetic genius and spiritual grandeur, how insolent the critics. Yet why should I express surprise? Was it not ever thus? It is the new hemlock – "legal insanity" – essential for men who see through the web of deceptions we call modern society. They did it to Trakl, now they do it to Pound. Who will be next, I wonder?' So wrote König to his father from his Washington house.

They decided to stay on, Frieda was writing, and Gorka's Fourth was at last to be presented in Dallas. Their Georgetown residence soon became the same kind of vortex of energies that the Königs were accustomed to in Europe, only here it seemed almost impossible to live a private life.

To meet meant to be reported and talked about in a way that was qualitatively different from in Europe. The outside view of one's activities was a kind of totalitarian critique of one's position in society and soon the Königs saw that if they were to be accepted it meant a radical reappraisal of their position or the kind of guarded silence that they had always refused to adopt. In some way they constantly found themselves being asked to make testimonial declarations of their ideological position. The greatest irony, to Frieda 'the joke' of American ideology, was anti-communism. They were to watch fascinated as during the 1950s the attempt at anti-communism swung to a defence of communism as being one of the 'rights' of free speech and so on. The fall of McCarthy seemed to the Königs more indicative of what was happening in the USA than the witchhunt that had preceded it. Again and in vain the Königs argued: 'Don't you see? This is not the real dialectic. Something else is happening. Another set of values is being set up and once it is established you will not know what has happened, you will only know what you are permitted to know.' As Johann König explained to them: 'Mass indoctrination goes in, as public debate, and comes back out, as privately formed opinion.'

Although there still was a traditional elite with

an established society of wealth and political influence as in England, the Königs earlier than others were conscious of the seismic shift in the top social echelons that would soon create a new power group and a new leadership in intellectual matters. But they were far from alone in their disapproval of bill after bill that to them clearly indicated openly that the much vaunted freedom and democracy built into their Constitution was without substance. Suspicious of Truman for his collaboration with the atomic scientists – Einstein and Oppenheimer were hailed as heroes and humanists! – they watched the message to Congress that was to be known as the Truman Doctrine place America irrevocably on the line Roosevelt had always wanted, and his Fair Deal was the son of the New Deal. To the Königs it meant that the ship of state, which was political governance, was being untied from its harbour of economic power until it floated a helpless and unfueled mass on open seas, visible, existent and powerless. The 1947 Taft-Hartley Act was already law and part of life in the America of the 1950s and the Eisenhower Doctrine merely the military confirmation of the newly designed imperialism. Against this turbulent and pessimistic backcloth the Königs pursued their intellectual interests and, with a small group of friends, deepened their understanding of how it was possible to see beyond the 'official history' and bypass the set of necessary dialectics, communism and capitalism, nations and international organizations, politics and economics, and to this, Frieda insisted, must be added the mythic separation of psychology and sociology.

There was not a musically aware public in America in the way there seemed to be in Europe and König began to long for his familiar landscape of music and musicians. In America they preferred him as a conductor than a composer and it came as a shock to König the day he realized that ten years had slipped by without his having composed anything. Yet he had not wasted his time, he had gathered as best he could all the works of Anton von Webern and immersed himself in his master's musical language and structural concepts and, most fascinating of all, his post-Schönbergian development. The result was his Fifth Symphony, bleak and deliberate, set within an uncompromising frame of technique that seemed to strip the music of all emotional content. The score looked more satisfactory than the sound, said his critics. To others it represented a new development, a new strength and a sign that he was saved from what seemed to some of his admirers that ever constant risk of Mahlerian emotional vulgarity which they had suspected in the Second, and detected in the Fourth.

By the 1960s the Königs had taken a house on Martha's Vineyard where their friends were mostly writers. Frieda was as popular as her husband was suspect. She was vivacious and always good to look at, necessary virtues in those circles, while she practised the magic art, or science as they all pretended, of psychiatry. She liked to say, 'It is not something you do, it is something you write!' They decided she was a liberal, and so acceptable, he was everything from a hopeless conservative to a bloody fascist. Since he would not enter into polemics or discussions, exchanging ignorances he called it, there was never any resolution to the König 'problem', his otherness, his silent rejection of the free-and-easy society that presented itself as the forefront of advanced civilization, 'how the future should be' the more militant declared. König could not be convinced. He had sat with Pound, and his release after thirteen years in a lunatic asylum was a bitter and fruitless end to the story. The damage had been done. 'They have won! They have released him to die, so they will not be blamed.' That was Gorka's viewpoint and he did not really want to talk about it. It made people uncomfortable. The Kennedy set charmed them but did not convert them to the myth of politics. What interested König was that Jack Kennedy thought something could be done. He really believed that political power could be wielded and that the Kennedy wealth and clout could protect them from the forces that might resist them. The confidence of the Kennedy set that not only things but great things could be done made him shiver. If they succeeded of course, in a very important way, his thesis was disproved. He was convinced that the power nexus barely interfaced with the official structures of public power, and then only aesthetically or theatrically. If Kennedy got in, and that was a mathematical roll of the electoral dice, then it implied to him only a postponement of what had to happen in the United States. The dice fell, just, in his favour. The next day the first great compromise took place. Johnson was to be his running-mate. It seemed as if König's disappointment had settled, seething in his gut, and the same night he was rushed to hospital and operated on for an emergency appendectomy.

As if the operation marked the end of a period for them the Königs decided to return to Europe. Two months later with the summer over, they packed up, Gorka, Frieda, and their two children, nine-year-old Anton and eight-year-old Eva, and set out for Freiburg and a reunion with Johann. Before they left they had to endure, as Gorka put it, another visit from Anna Sorel. As the glamorous grandmother she insisted on photographs with the children and despite the complaints of their parents she managed to captivate and entrance young Eva who had never seen anything so fabulous and mythical as this creature, brilliantly preserved in time by all the means available to science and yoga. To her public her legs were famous. To herself her intellect was famous. To her lovers her cooking was famous. To her granddaughter she was a woman who had proved to the world that she existed, and this, as she later wrote, was her one aching desire.

From a musical point of view König's sense of alienation in America finally produced the luminous classical modernism of his Fifth. From an intellectual point of view the meeting with Pound certainly produced a new vision of civilization and its driving force. It was from then that he began to explore the monetary system as being the underlying dynamic of a society and thus of its historical destiny, but more deeply he saw that unless the philosophical basis of the society was safe, the society was not safe. He discovered, as he put it, that with the halting of the philosophical discourse that was the German heritage, began the rape of the world through a usury that a pure metaphysic would never permit. There is no doubt that the mature symphonies are a result of reflections on that theme and the dialogue he had at last been able to open up with his father. As he so movingly wrote to Johann König, 'The father of my music is philosophy.'

5.

The Königs' return to Freiburg marks the starting point of the composer's 'period of synthesis'. In one interview he likened his understanding about the dynamic relationship between music and ideas to the literary metaphor of the 'Bead Game' imagined by Hermann Hesse. In another, unfortunately unrecorded broadcast, he talked openly of the idea of symphony as philosophy, presenting the argument that Beethoven's innovation was precisely his capacity to describe musically a world-view and a set of values and that to talk of programmatic intention was to obfuscate the profound revolution that Beethoven had brought about in musical expression.

Gorka had been shocked by the trivialization of his mother, which he was not prepared to blame on her character or lack of it so much as an inevitable historical process that had been the price she had paid for her defection from her homeland and people in 1939. It occurred to him that she had known an identity crisis more than a political one, for she had changed her name to Sorenson on entering a theatrical career and to Sorel on her espousal of a Hollywood one. While his mother seemed to have lost the glow of her earlier days as preserved in his memory, his father on his return made a deep impression on the mature composer. He recognized the gift of consistency, and continual inner dialogue, in his father's development. He had never ceased growing and questioning, and most importantly, re-defining what he knew and had always known. 'You have not been consistent with your innermost being unless you are accused of having changed your position and again accused of having changed your position. The argument against the validity of the philosopher as being that he changes his mind is the proof of his integrity and constancy,' wrote Johann König to his son.

The Königs settled into their new house and became again the threesome they had been before the departure of the younger ones for America, through their constant reunions with Johann, living in and out of each other's houses. Also they seemed to inspire each other to work, and simultaneously the three of them embarked on new creations. In 1962 Gorka began the Sixth, his great choral symphony, the first attempt at a synthesis between Wagner and Webern, in a large-scale work that avoided the Mahlerian trap of meandering length and thin texture, of emotional effect minus inner architecture.

Frieda was writing her controversial and political

work on psychiatry, Fashions in Madness: a Study in Autism. In this long and difficult work she combined clinical study and aphoristic comment, which perhaps more than anything else revealed the impact that her father-in-law was having on the Königs, for, just as Gorka's music changed through their dialogue, so did her style and method of expression. Her thesis that each epoch produced a style of madness in harmony or dissonance with its method of creating ultimate stress implied a direct link between the world of the psyche and the world of politics. She outlined what she called 'the Ophelia Complex' as the form of madness of the medieval society where the victim was almost always a woman, and her technique of inner survival was to 'drift' from reality. Her other example of this complex was Lady Macbeth for she suggested this type of madness dominated until the Renaissance. The industrial revolution brought what she called 'Gothic madness' or schizophrenia with its highly dramatic splitting of the personality. Here she suggested Mary Shelley's Frankenstein myth as embodying the process, which was that the schizophrenic 'other' was a monstrous creation, a monstrous lovable creation of its unacknowledged master. This was also defined as a classical form of schizophrenia by Stevenson in his Dr Jekyll legend. Frieda saw autism as the robot-age's form of madness, a deeper sickness indicating a more alienated society. Her clinical study of the American woman psychiatrist with the autistic child was one of the most disturbing and powerful parts of the book which made an immediate impact on a public far beyond the specialized realm of psychiatric literature, despite her uncompromisingly technical style and vocabulary. As part of the König household she had learned to make no compromises to please the public and she was rewarded by a response from intelligent people who showed that the quest for knowledge still illuminated her country.

Johann König had started his magnum opus which was to crown his life's remarkable achievements, his long and profound study of Nietzsche. 'The Nietzsche Dialogues' were constructed as a series of talks between the great Master and the twentieth-century pupil, Johann König.

For Frieda and her book, recognition and success. For Gorka with the launching of his Sixth a musical triumph but to him worthless because of the stubborn refusal of the public to 'hear' the message. They want a Mahlerian frisson, they will not work through to the vision – this was his complaint. To Johann with the publication of the first volume of his master-work, it was as if he had not written it. It fell on a critical and public void.

Nobody wanted to read about Nietzsche. 'Quite simply,' said Johann König, 'he has not been de-nazified.' Gorka was more aggressive, 'And now they have burned his books!' Frieda's response to the rejection of the philosopher's work was more ironic, 'I would rather go to hell with Nietzsche than to heaven with Sigmund Freud.' The Königs were still out of tune with their time, in conflict, alone in both fame and isolation.

The reception of the Sixth Symphony in 1964 was a clear indication of how unprepared the public were for its political theme. Musically it was hailed as a masterpiece, everybody praised it, and yet, today, reading the critics and the material written on it at the time, it emerges that the intellectuals as much as the public were distant from the theme. König's choice for his first choral work of the text of the Usury Canto by Ezra Pound came as a total surprise to a society at that time utterly involved in other issues, and quite unaware of any moral dialogue suggesting that the ills of the society were caused by its monetary system. To attack usury was, in the 1960s, either considered medievalist or plain right-wing romantic.

'The astonishing thing is,' wrote König to Frieda, 'that nobody knows what usury is, not even the people who tell me I should not waste time with the matter. Usury, in fact, is a forbidden subject not an outmoded one.'

'The concept of interest as a crime has still to return to Europe. People think they are radical if they suggest limiting interest, abolition is still unthinkable. That such an action should also be accompanied by a return to a bi-metal and commodities economy is beyond the imagination – but for how long? Sooner or later the illogicality of the current monetary system has to burst upon the world – but when? Do not be surprised at public incomprehension. You have baffled them and they cannot escape the theme now. The Usury Canto is accepted as "poetry", your Sixth, the Contra Usura, is accepted as "music", the content cannot be avoided for ever. It will be acted on, so was the Ring, remember?' wrote back Frieda.

'The Contra Usura' Symphony was duly performed everywhere without ever a murmur of intellectual confrontation with its passionately pleaded and lyrically expressed argument. The comparison which is closest to the work – the critical reception of Pound – is the most pertinent. A whole industry of Pound criticism had poured from the universities. Everyone dutifully condemned his politics either as some kind of poetic folly with licence or as downright insanity. Nobody, but nobody took on the Cantos as a political statement. The thesis that sound money was the foundation of a sound society was still ignored or considered irrelevant.

The Pound text awakened again the witch-hunting, although it had never really stopped. The 1958 trials against Nazis had come as a shock to the Königs, then in America, but they followed them closely, amazed at the audacity of trying people for actions performed twenty years before. In 1960 a cabinet minister had been forced to resign because of his National Socialist past, and a year after the Sixth had been performed in Germany a Bill prolonging the statute of limitations on National Socialist activities prosecutions was passed in the Bundestag. König was again to face a press inquisition. He could only reiterate his view that the right-left dialectic was false, that political structures were divorced from monetary power, that democracy far from being an instrument of freedom was an instrument of control by non-nationalist money-based structures. In the end it seemed as if they got bored persecuting him. Some more observant people began to comment that they could no longer quote him as he was talking too good sense to be anything but dangerous.

Gorka König's Seventh was, like his Fifth, a piece

of 'pure music', or so the critics said. König insisted it was polemical, political, and philosophical. It resulted in a flurry of critical examination because of its renowned composer's insistence that it presented an agony of man struggling for liberation from the dark monetarist forces in the well-lit and comfortable prison of democracy. From that year, 1966, König began his active campaigning against interest-based economy and calling for a return to a gold-silver economy, spot-trading and an abolition of the cancerous growth of futures trading which had not yet emerged as a major force, or threat, on the stock exchanges of the West.

He declared himself a radical, but confused those who were aware of his own anti-communist views. He declared that communism and interest-non-value-money capitalism were the world status quo. In opposing them he was a radical. Why is it, he would passionately argue, that the only two countries not threatened internally by revolutionary movements are Russia and America yet they are both statist monoliths?

His attack on monetarism and world banking was ahead of the world's consciousness about the problem of the exploding debt system, not just in the Third World but by the USA, debts owed not country to country but to supra-national banking institutions whose leadership, as König never tired of pointing out, was appointed by no existing body of people according to the so-sacred principles of democracy. Power in the world is in the hands of unknown men, elected by no constituency, against all the vaunted tenets of democracy, which in the end is the instrument to guarantee the inaccessibility of monetary power to governmental bodies.

This polemic was totally obliterated by the so-called student movement in the late 1960s. Yet König went on arguing and pleading his case. He was convinced that the 'student uprising' was but one part of a long-term programme creating a shift in the underlying money-flow system, in order to open it up for future profits. Branded as irrelevant and a crypto-fascist, König's music still seemed to make an enormous and positive impact on its public.

By 1970 the family was reduced. Eva finally got her way and was allowed to go to Hollywood and stay with her grandmother, now a 'living legend' who did not like to be photographed. Anton had left home too, determined to pursue a career as a soldier. His entry into military academy had surprised and delighted both his father, and grandfather. In August 1970 the Moscow Treaty was signed and that was followed in December by the Warsaw

Treaty, the two agreements in effect legalizing and 'finalizing' European borders, particularly that of the Oder-Neisse Line and that between the B.R.D. and the D.D.R. König had just finished his Eighth Symphony, but he was moved immediately to start work on another major symphonic work, the monumental Ninth, which he entitled 'A German Symphony'.

The enormous edifice of his Ninth is all the more remarkable for its immaculate inner structure. Built mathematically in a taut framework it manages within that to explore so many different musical languages and ideas as to be almost too dense to follow. He leads his listener, captivated and moved, as if attending a master class, through German music from Bach right up to Webern. His Eighth by contrast is an almost elegant piece written to delight, filled with a radiant and joyful energy it seems to presage the masterpiece of his Tenth.

König's Ninth placed him in the forefront of all living composers and re-affirmed inescapably the central role of German music in western civilization and thought. Asked to define greatness he had replied, 'In a thinker – my father. In an artist – von Karajan. In a writer – Ernst Jünger.' 'And in a man?' the interviewer had asked. König's reply was made with a radiant and confident smile: 'The

Übermensch has still to come.' That statement revealed something new about König, his main interest was now philosophy not monetarism. He did not reject his view of usury but was convinced that it could not be imposed on the world, or rather the world could not free itself from the curse of an interest-non-value money system without an absolutely correct fundamental basis in its philosophy. He was also convinced that while all profound dialogue in the philosophical realm had been deliberately severed with the downfall of German hegemony in Europe it could only reconnect its continuity by taking up the dialogue started by his father in the Nietzsche papers he had written. 'This is the core of dynamic politics,' Frieda had confirmed to him in a long letter. 'I wish to be near you again, I sense that you are becoming more and more a private and perhaps even reclusive person and I want to share these precious days with you.'

In that significant letter König's wife confirms her husband's withdrawal, or the beginning of his withdrawal, from the world, a movement or inclination which was to terminate, it would seem, with his occultation. The years 1965 to 1975 were years of tremendous productivity in which the composer was to produce four major symphonies. The Seventh was finished in 1966, the

Eighth in 1970. The Ninth received its first public performance in 1973, symbolically, in Berlin. Ironically, it was after its rapturous reception by a public enormously sympathetic to his courageous and still unpopular patriotism, that König began almost entirely to disappear from public view.

König and Frieda returned to Freiburg and then prepared for one last family duty. They had arranged a tour of the great German-speaking universities for Johann. They had planned that in each one he would deliver a paper from the as yet unpublished 'Nietzsche Dialogues'. Inevitably, with the passing years and the sheer strength of the philosophical tradition in Germany, which despite inroads had not by any means perished at the hands of its enemies, there were many people not only who wished to hear what Johann König had to say but who wished to honour him for a lifetime devoted to the highest thinking. So in 1974 the König family began their tour of the Germanic world, opening again a discourse that had been, by political dictate, or by social stigmatism, effectively silenced through neglect and outright hostility.

At the elite and almost secret, or let us say private, level of society his radical re-appraisal of Nietzsche made devastating impact. Publicly, and as much as his visits were noted by the press he was submitted to the usual denigration, the cold rejection informing the public they did not have to worry since the thought of this man was devalued by his stigmatic relationship with Naziism, and thus even his apparent discourses on metaphysics and methodology were not to be considered relevant to the new humanism. Nevertheless what Gorka König achieved by the tour was what he had desired, a re-affirmation of his father's greatness before a new generation of young Germans who had not been asked to pursue their heritage of being the philosophers of western civilization and its masters intellectually for centuries. In private meetings with students Johann König again and again stressed to his eager listeners their duty to take up the discourse where it had been abandoned. He called on them to hold to the Germanic heritage and language – High German is the natural language of philosophy he declared – and most of all not to abandon their political imperative, the reunification of the Fatherland. He would not talk in the language of the current dialectic and at last he found an audience who was itself tired of it. Racism and anti-racism is a false dialectic, he insisted, East-West conflict is a false dialectic. He could only offer the high ground, recaptured but bare, of metaphysical vision. Once you have established a healthy metaphysics, he insisted, you will move relentlessly to a set of actions that will change the world.

In 1975 Johann König died and was buried in Freiburg. After the funeral of his father Gorka saw to the publication of his final text which Johann had given to him from his deathbed. The work was a short monograph entitled 'The necessity to abandon Averroes and recover Ibn Rushd: a philosophical enquiry into a deception'. The argument was that Aristotelian debate and method had been derailed by the absorption of the Thomist and Judaeo-Christian pseudo-scholarship that resulted in their 'readings' of Ibn Rushd and that it was imperative to re-connect the wholistic thinking of Ibn Rushd who saw philosophical discourse as a subject to be conducted in utter freedom devoid of theological and moralistic revaluations while at the same time accepting the legal framework of Islam as the basis for the governance of society both in justice and in worship, to the modern dilemma, a dilemma caused in part by that prejudicial religious tyranny of rabbis and priests over philosophical dialogue.

Immediately after his father's death König began to work with great speed and intensity on what has proved to be his final symphony, the Tenth, final, that is, as far as we know. The symphony came to be known as 'Das Heitere' but in fact, written under the enumeration on the title page of his manuscript he had written: 'Die wissende Heiterkeit'. Knowing joy was to be his last musical testament. Again he insisted on the first performance taking place in Berlin, and this time the opposition was from the USSR who feared it would be used to trigger some kind of nationalistic uprising and again awaken the urge for unification that they, with America, had worked so hard to stifle. It was somehow inevitable that his Tenth would also be a Choral Symphony. What no one expected was the astonishing use of the human voices and the more extraordinary use of the text, this time a text even more remote and difficult because built up with phrases, words and sentences from his father's 'Nietzsche Dialogues'. The exultant final affirmation of knowing joy after the journey through anguish and darkness inevitably brought people's minds to Beethoven's Ninth of which it was an undoubted child. Yet the sheer musical originality and final sublime serenity was uniquely and unquestionably König's.

One week after the Berlin premiere Gorka and Frieda König had disappeared. They have not been sighted or heard of since. No form of communication has come from them and no message was left by them. The books and manuscripts had vanished from their house which had been legally passed to Anton. If he knew he did not say, and if he mourned he did not cry. From a biographical point of view there

only remains speculation and the confirmation
that Gorka König's 'disappearance' is somehow
in harmony with his musical and philosophical
career. After the Tenth Symphony his silence takes
on a metaphysical majesty that cannot be denied.
It is not a theatrical gesture but a final closing
to an extraordinary life. Nobody who knew the
Königs would for one moment consider suicide as
a solution, certainly a dual one seems unthinkable
for two people so dedicated to courage and the
quest for truth. Gorka König is silent. The music
remains. Or if you like, the music has stopped, and
the life remains. May God bless him with knowing
joy, wherever he may be.

Chapter Two

The Ten Symphonies

First Symphony (1938)

The First Symphony, known as the Wagner Symphony, of Gorka König had a historic first public performance in Munich attended by Adolf Hitler and the leaders of the National Socialist government. To write a symphonic tribute to Wagner which opens and closes with his own music could, in a first work by a young composer, have been a disastrous and hubristic act, only the sheer originality of the intervening music turns the audacity into a fitting and serious comment both on its subject and his own central idea. Even now that audiences know what to expect, the effect of the close of the symphony remains thrilling.

The symphony's opening is none other than the famous closing bars of Götterdämmerung. To

open not only a symphony but one's work as a
composer with music of such absolute finality as
the end of the great Ring Cycle which declares
the total destruction of the old order, of a
whole world, and the serene end with value and
wealth returned to its source in the primal waters,
immediately puts the educated listener in a state of
suspense. What can possibly follow? A measured
silence separates König's music from Wagner's in
a mark of respect which nevertheless integrates
the opening into the total statement of the work.
A series of muted trumpet calls increase in 'near-
ness' and tempo, yet while it makes us strain to
hear some of the Siegfried motif the texture of the
sound is crisp and fresh. We have entered another
world. Woodwind awaken to new life, insistent
and complex. In a sudden gush of full orchestral
sound the trumpets return ff with an energetic
rhythm. Once the utterly original texture of the
music has imposed itself on the listener it plunges
into a peasant dance, alpine, bucolic, and with
a kind of Brucknerian simplicity, yet still with a
modern tonality that is unmistakable. The country
atmosphere is sustained by the use of cor anglais
and cow bells until one fears the grotesque, but
the composer is clearly in command. The movement ends with a calming of the orchestra, and
a low repetition of the dance theme, now on two
trombones, across which an utterly unrelated and

martial message imposes itself from timpani and side drum, forceful and virile and coming to an abrupt end.

The Scherzo and Trio have a Beethoven-like construction which reminds one of the composer's youth and inexperience, it seems structurally to be a pure conservatoire piece of composition. What sustains it is the dazzling control of orchestral expression. An extended fugato with richly textured string scoring seems to be about to open into a Tchaikovsky-like sequence, but the originality of voice is sustained. König launches into a series of rich harmonies which throw out set after set of simple-phrase melodies and in the end it is the strict adherence to classical form imposing itself on this crude material that gives it its nobility and emotional force.

The third movement, Moderato, opens with pizzicato strings pp and then flute and drum re-introduce the martial theme that terminated the first movement. A tension builds up between this and a new turbulent swelling wave of sound that passes through the strings starting with violas, and then cellos, then the pizzicato theme that was whispered at the opening is taken up ominously by the basses, finally the violins enter carrying this wave of sound to its climax and as it subsides the entry of clarinets and oboes unifies the two themes in a complex fugal pattern.

The last movement, Allegro Maestoso, opens with emphatic repeated chords which recall the end of Beethoven's Fifth, but they open up into a full musical statement that emerges as a noble funeral march using the full orchestra in an unrelenting volume of sound. Eventually it dissolves and shimmers, transposing itself as it diminishes until it becomes, miraculously, the opening of Rheingold and the Ring Cycle, and as Wagner's famous chord extends itself, swelling and growing into life, suddenly and thrillingly, the phrase held by the twin trumpets at the start of the symphony flashes across the great chord first from the piccolo clarinet and then from the piccolo itself, shrill and vanishing, high and bright, until the chord has vanished and one last trill pierces the new silence

Second Symphony (1940)

König's Second Symphony in B does not have the emotional excitement of his first, but it does display such mastery of its material and it is endowed with so much youthful vigour and energy that, perhaps because of rather than despite its lack of originality, it proves to be a most sympathetic work to listen to and it is always enthusiastically received, yet it never has been taken seriously by König enthusiasts who tend, despite an obligatory loyalty to the First, to consider the König Canon as beginning with the Third, purists would say with the Fifth.

The first movement, Allegro con brio, opens with an energetic and buoyant theme on the violins which is then passed between solo flute and oboe. Trumpets enter with a second, playful almost jazz-like theme, and in the interplay between the two subjects the trumpet syncopation enhances the modernistic flavour of the work. The whole orchestra expand the exchange into a full statement of vigorous force. A superb and extended motif from the horns brings the movement to a sudden and unexpected end, like an unfinished sentence.

The Adagio is beautiful and has become deservedly popular as a piece on its own. The whole movement is uniquely in the hands of the woodwind section and its haunting melody is passed among them in a complex interweaving of harmonies and thin scoring that finally fades out until the plaintive and puzzling contrapuntal question and answer between cor anglais and clarinets again seems to halt in mid-phrase, uncompleted.

The Scherzo is formal and heavily scored. Its melodic simplicity is refreshing after the Honegger-like harmonies of the second movement. The full pulse of the Scherzo has a very distinctive character, immediately putting the German listener on home ground so to speak, firm Brahmsian ground.

The Largo that closes the symphony is broad and heroic in mood. It recapitulates the two main themes that opened the first movement and then introduces exquisite echoes of the Adagio with its melodies reversed now as if decoded. After a long passage that seems to deal harmonically with some of the problems of the Largo the whole orchestra takes up again the opening theme only for it, in turn, to be transformed into a slow march. Finally, the horns enter with their unfinished thematic material and it is resolved, perhaps crudely but vigorously in a dynamic flourish that seems to ensure applause.

Third Symphony (1945)

The Symphony No.3 in E flat Major received its first performance in Stuttgart in 1950. The sombre E flat Major chord that opens the Third is very different from the Wagnerian ending of the First. Here, in this powerfully moving and darkly elegiac work, König emerges for the first time as a serious voice in European music. Gone is the brilliant boy of the First and the talented but dutiful student of the Second. This, musically, is König entering into manhood.

The symphony begins with an ominous shuddering of violins and timpani then taken up by the violas. A second idea emerges with horns and timpani but this is interrupted by a series of crashing chords, and with their C Major force the music has moved out beyond its opening key. Still the opening intensity of the work has survived this onslaught and a grimly agitated chattering of strings that demands almost violent bowing continues over a hundred bars. A flourish of brass precedes a long superbly scored passage using the full orchestra, brass still dominant. Trumpets announce the major theme of the first movement, sweeping and aggressive, it is examined by each section of the orchestra in canon. Side drums and then bass drum in turn cut across this great stream of sound until it is as if the orchestra had split in two, which it in fact does. With dissonances of a profound emotional force the orchestra now embarks on a double fugue, superbly constructed. The pages of the score are themselves satisfying in their symmetry. With the formal resolution of the fugal pattern the movement ends with a classical decisiveness.

The macabre yet jocular Allegretto is short and shocking. It contains only one musical idea presented first by the percussion and then by pizzicato violas as it increases in tempo like a danse macabre. One critic called it skeletons rattling and sabres clashing. Xylophone and clarinets handle the climax and the demented dance comes to an abrupt exhausted end.

König is so clear in this symphony about what he wants to say that we do not argue about this reversal that places the Andante before the Adagio. He is writing a threnody for Germany and a defeated humanity. Programmatically some have seen the first three movements as the last three stages of the war. Firstly, the full ferocious might of the Wehrmacht and the blitzkrieg. Secondly the wild dance of death and thirdly the final sacrifice, the last heroic days of the war. König himself never commented on the work except in musical terms.

The first statement is a long relentless march introduced by the trombones and taken over by side drums and plucked strings. It builds into a great wall of sound implicating the full orchestra capped by powerful, slow pulsing on the bass drum. Strings which are not at first even identifiable in the storm introduce another melody, a funeral march of a totally different emotional calibre to the military march in the first half of the movement. This melody insinuates itself on the 'war march', subduing it, in some of the most complex and original scoring in all König's writing. It takes over and unifies the orchestra, rejecting dissonance, until it is one harmonized and majestic funeral march. A solo flute cuts across it, fluttering after its own exquisite melody, higher and higher, like a lark rising.

The Adagio that follows seems to announce that despite the 'bird of peace' which closes the Andante, the suffering is not over. The Finale of 'The Dark Night' opens with cellos almost sobbing a lament. The bowing is strictly marked and the unison of the opening with violas and basses taking up the mourning is both aurally and visually moving. No percussion is employed in this movement. The drums of war are silenced.

As if this grief-stricken sound was not enough to touch the core of our beings, the low woodwind instruments enter with another even more poignant melody. Material from the opening movement is passed between strings and woodwind but the lament ignores it and continues. A third element is introduced by muted trumpets and horns which in turn offer up their lamentation. Almost stifled trombones fill out the rich sonority of the three laments which are now woven together into one web of sound. Subtle dissonances come and go, always relentlessly smoothed out, until a solo violin enters with its own richly phrased contribution. The violin seems to subdue the orchestra but then one by one the other strings, the woodwind and the brass submit to its lead and join in the one heart-breaking elegy. This whole movement has been so designed and scored that despite the emotional impact it soars above the slightest hint of sentimentality. The end produces the coup de grace. When the music falls to silence a solo piano, pedalled, with slow considered phrasing, makes the final statement. Meditative, sober, and with that grave nobility of the mightiest Beethoven sonatas, König gives us three minutes of pure 'classical' music composed in a timeless style, majestic and detached. It is as if in these last moments König is reaching out beyond the tragedy of the war to remind the German people and the world of their true greatness and nobility.

Fourth Symphony (1950)

The Fourth Symphony marks the period of König's exile in 'barren Amerika' as he called it, echoing Pound's use of the 'k' when he wished to indicate that his own country was in enemy hands.

He was not to hear it for five years and we know that he worked on it more than once during that time. He wrote to his father, 'Its construction is shallow and its shape all wrong. I've revised it over and over again but I still cannot get it to come out right.' It was finally performed in Dallas where it was given a rapturous reception by the public but not the critics.

The first movement is thematic in style but with too complex an interweaving of its three main subjects. The conventional sonata form dominates the movement but the obtuse musical language and the inter-cutting, to use an appropriate cinematic expression, between themes is disconcerting. The accusation of Mahlerian pastiche is due partly to this but more to a certain lapse of emotional taste or authenticity so unlike König's great symphonies. The first movement is over-scored and it seems to compensate with breadth of sound for its missing depth of ideas. König's usual vitality does not offset the sense of lack of direction and emotional line.

The second movement is rambling with long chamber orchestra passages with solo flights among, first, the strings, and then the brass. This again recalls the unstructured Mahler rather than the indulgent Mahler, and suggests that the tale told of König's father exclaiming at a New York Mahler concert, 'Somebody answer the 'phone!' would be more appropriate here.

The Adagio and Finale that terminate the piece reveal König's almost Schubertian facility of melodic invention but little more. It is as if in this movement he had retreated into his national tradition too late. Its orderliness of construction is undermined by its dense orchestral texture, modern and over-ripe. From an analytical and aesthetic point of view the Fourth Symphony simply does not work, and even the public popularity which it still enjoys, seems undeserved.

Fifth Symphony (1960)

König's Fifth Symphony is dedicated to Anton von Webern. It, too, was first performed in Dallas, in 1960. There is no doubt that with this symphony Gorka König became recognized as one of the great symphonists not only of our time but of western music. The piece is a profound and closely wrought meditation on Webernian matters of form and content. It is here, stripped to its musically bare bones, that we meet for the first time the masterly composer of the next five symphonies. It is as if in this homage to his master he has laid bare the architectural principles with which he will build his own idiosyncratic masterpieces.

The Fifth is in three movements played without a break. It is not based on a fixed tonal centre and the progressive analysis of its opening statements are examined with mathematical precision. The composer achieves an almost unbearable intensity right from the beginning and sustains it to the end. Complex inversions, retrograde progressions and sudden transpositions keep the music dramatically urgent and the schematic formality assures that the predetermined end is never allowed to escape despite the intricacy of the journey.

König leads his listeners with measured exactitude into a zone of bleak and arid musicality which becomes through the sheer weight and conviction of the structural argument, so harmonically controlled that its emotional effect far from being diminished is guaranteed with an absolute predictability.

The composer has created in the Bachian and mathematical sense a piece of perfect music, pure intellectually and melodically. In the end the impact is sublime, elevating and spiritual. There is nothing like it in the canon of König's symphonic works, yet there is no doubt that in some way it is his musical testament. His master would have been as proud of him as we are grateful to him.

Sixth Symphony (1964)

König's Sixth Symphony marked his return to Europe after his prolonged stay in the United States. Started in 1962 it was not completed until 1964 when it received its first performance in Germany. While in the Fifth König had for the first time utilized the serial techniques of his teacher, Webern, he had also submitted to a strictly disciplined application of them, like a student absorbing the method in order to make it his own. From the Sixth Symphony onwards he was to go beyond that rigidity, and some would say sterility, freeing his music from absolute formality but always with such a theoretical foundation that he could utilize the narrow disciplines of the style when he needed them to provide that mathematical structuralism that suited his most profound statements in a manner which showed that he was as much a Bachian as a Webernian, but then in his estimation so was Webern and this was his strength and his contribution and the reason he was important to German music in a manner Schönberg was not, although the latter had led his own student to the path that would purify modern music of its decadent longing to remain under the shadow of the nineteenth-century giants.

It is the impact of familiarity of expression in a post-serialist mode, by a composer who had absorbed the significance of Webern's last compositions, and who had found his way back to the Bachian systems, which gives the Sixth its particular mood at once modern and anxious, in a style that was to influence his contemporaries profoundly, and at the same time distant, serene and exalted in that specifically Baroque voice that makes this symphony at times sound almost like a Lutheran cantata performed in a local church with inadequate means rather than a piece scored for a complex vocal and instrumental array and demanding the highest level of conducting.

König composed two fully choral symphonies and one (the Ninth) with a choral movement. It is interesting that there seems neither progression nor relationship in his use of the choir in these three symphonies. In the Sixth the choir narrates and comments on the text. In the Ninth a sophisticated statement is being made on Beethoven. In the Tenth König has reached a synthesis of voices and instruments that sets that work apart from all his previous compositions.

The text of the Sixth consists of the famous 'Usury Canto' from Ezra Pound's Pisan Cantos, that is, Canto XLV, as well as Canto LI, which also speaks of usury. The work is in four movements. The first movement opens with a fugal arrangement using half of the strings, woodwind and brass in a chamber-sized sound, bucolic and vigorous. It presents, as it were, the wholesome sound of music belonging to an integrated society uncorrupted by the usury which is the symphony's subject. After a brief silence the drums begin a long passage at first heavy and deep, then moving through the battery of the percussion the message becomes more military and aggressive, more strident. The violas enter, pizzicato, followed by the cellos in a shuddering and ominous theme. The tonality is astonishing in that it somehow manages to maintain the atmosphere of a cantata from the Bach period while the texture of the sound remains disturbingly modern. The entry of the brass with a new declamatory theme announces the 'With Usura' subject which dominates the rest of the movement and is to reappear in each subsequent movement in various forms and sonorities. The poem itself is first taken up by a heldentenor and later a coloratura. The choir handle the annunciatory 'With Usura' and then contrapuntally follow a solo voice in the most intricate and ravishing series of patterned sound sung on an open 'ah' vowel. The urgency and dramatic nature of the message is underlined by the rich scoring that accompanies the solo singing utilizing the full orchestra and reaching a full golden sound when the choir take up the text:

Came not by usura Angelico;
came not Ambrosio Praedis,
Came no church of cut stone signed:
Adamo me fecit.
Not by usura St Trophime
Not by usura Saint Hilaire,
Usura rusteth the chisel
It rusteth the craft and the craftsman
It gnaweth the thread of the loom
None learneth to weave gold in her pattern;
Azure hath a canker by usura;
cramoisi is unbroidered
Emerald findeth no Memling
Usura slayeth the child in the womb
It stayeth the young man's courting
It hath brought palsey to bed, lyeth
between the young bride and her bridegroom
                       CONTRA NATURAM

The symphony moves quickly into its second movement which is dominated by a dialogue between the choir and the full orchestra uniquely dealing with the 'contra naturam' subject. Here again that unique quality of control over his musical framework which so separates König from his contemporaries is what gives power and emotional force to this music. In so much modern music one hears such a personal, such a neurotic voice, the composer by the techniques he has adopted seems to reveal himself, vulnerable and defenceless, not in the romantic sense in which Tchaikovsky bares his anguish, for that is due to a melodic confession, rather the problem of the modern composer is his lack of thought and it reveals itself in a harmonic confession. His statement lacks a ground, a foundation, it is too alone and isolated from society even when the composer tries to take a communist posture. With König there is a dynamic and almost hearty identity with his own tradition and his own people, his Teutonic background (in the linguistic sense) seems to confirm for him a sense of belonging. He is not just writing from his own personal convictions but is continuing a musical and indeed a philosophical dialogue that has been the mainstream of western civilization and that is why one 'hears' Bach and Wagner in his music when, in fact, they cannot be identified in the score. It was this quality which was to find its fruition in his anthological review of the tradition in his Ninth Symphony. And all this development in his writing had its beginning in that deliberately copied usage of the great E flat Rheingold chord that ended his first Symphony.

The third movement is a meditation on the lines which open Canto LI:

Shines
in the mind of heaven God
who made it
more than the sun
In our eye.

This highly pitched and exalted phrasing makes enormous vocal demands on the soloists who dominate the full orchestral exploration of this theme. The music shimmers in the highest registers of all the instruments until it is almost unbearable but with an unbearableness such as Rilke spoke of when defining beauty as that which nearly destroys us.

The next movement deals with the main body of the same Canto's text. Here the whole work opens up in a quite unexpected way. König had carefully selected the two cantos which repeat deliberately some of the same images and ideas. So now, in their second presentation König daringly moves the whole musical atmosphere away from that Baroque styling that is actually pure Webernian method into a more open application of his system. While there is no hint, as I have indicated above, of a sonority borrowed from another composer, König shows his special genius for learning from his masters, so that one recalls another composer while failing to 'find' him in the harmonics. What happens with the third movement is that the choral narration takes on the Wagnerian technique by which the orchestra expresses and creates the psychological and emotional texture that the poetry is expressing so that we experience the idea. If one were to say what the movement is like, one would say that it is like the Norns' breaking of the thread of destiny, or Erda being awakened to tell her story, yet it is with a luminously fine and original sound texture that is not at all Wagnerian. One could say that it is the very first extension of the Wagnerian concept of psychologising situations by musical means since the Ring. The movement is structured on the duologue between the two soloists whose exposition is extended to considerable lengths by the orchestral zone that is set up around their narration. One of the beauties and rewarding complexities of this third movement is the way in which the precise and formal musical statements of the first movement spread and reveal themselves when re-iterated in the text of Canto LI.

The final movement deals with the first part of the last section of Canto LI.

That hath the light of the doer, as it were
a form cleaving to it.
Deo similis quodam modo
hic intellectus adeptus
Grass; nowhere out of place.
Thus speaking in Königsberg
Zwischen die Völkern erzielt wird
a modus vivendi.

The fourth movement is brief and as formal in structure as the beginning, drawing in after the expansive force of the third movement. Again, and to great effect, König uses the inner orchestra, chamber sized, making the sound and the texture of emotion finer and more controlled. He even plays a light joke with his public in allowing the coloratura a lingering and caressing time over 'Thus speaking in Königsberg' in a manner which delighted Pound as much as it does his audience.

The tremendous success of this symphony has always been frustrating for König – for while it has remained popular its theme has stubbornly refused to challenge its enthusiastic public. Until recently, one might add, for the subject of usury has moved from being an elite concern known only to the very rich and some academics to being the stuff of post-Marxist revolution in a world that calls for change beyond what can be provided by capitalism-communism.

Seventh Symphony (1966)

In his Seventh Symphony the mature König chooses to make a further statement, this time in purely musical terms. Whatever 'content' it may have has to be absorbed in terms of its musicality and impact on the listener. There is no programme to clarify its meanings and yet the composer at the same time has made it known that he considers it a work of polemical engagement. It is from this work that much musicological debate has stemmed, for here ideally one can examine whether in fact there is any way in which the choice of key, the harmonics, the scoring of a symphonic work can elicit from the audience a response of allegiance to a set of ideas, or feelings of an identifiable nature.

The outer form is uncompromisingly classical, four movements architecturally built to scale, a predictable outer frame whose inner design is full of surprises like a reconditioned and modernized castle. Or to change the metaphor it is like a beautiful face in repose, perfect bone structure and poise, inwardly full of ambiguities, criticism, sarcasm, irony and rage.

The Allegro opens with trumpets announcing a theme of robust vigour. Timpani and bassoons come in swiftly to contest the healthy opening. A negative theme from the woodwind comes to us protesting, its character piercing and tormented. In this first movement we taste the new harmonics of König in their full confidence. Where before he liked simple resolution leading to full chords and open phrasing here he enters into more complex, ambiguous adventures, with dissonance, incomplete chords, broken phrases and unresolved harmonies. The musical language is post-Webernian and completely König's own.

A lyrical theme emerges from the violins, a long flowing passage of 100 bars, and it is this beautiful sequence that throughout the movement has to 'fight for its life', even fragments of it wriggle into motion throughout the whole symphony. It is here that König's alienation first declares itself. The argument is conducted in purely musical language. The violins are 'broken up', set against each other, interrupted by fierce cutting energy from the brass led by the horns who mockingly 'reject' the message of the violins. The woodwind come in with a frivolous dance, lively and entertaining but stubbornly refusing the persistent attempts of the strings to return to serious matters. The struggle ends with the silencing of the violins, the triumph of the brass, in turn threatened by the flighty clarinets.

The Adagio has the same style of interrupted proceedings. The classical achievement is again being trivialized, swept aside, for a vulgar and worthless alternative. A noble melody on the brass, muted and sober, is this time contested by the oboes and the flutes. The same dissonances and transpositions sweep aside the attempt at a traditional movement. This time, allied to shaking the structural base of the harmonics, the style is jeopardized. The thin sound of Alban Berg, or cheaper still, that of Eisler or Weill, insinuates itself. They 'conquer' the brass and the trombones surrender in dying phrases their place before the new force of the reedy decadence and its new nostalgic lament. The Adagio ends with xylophone and piano taking over.

The Scherzo is, as it were, a total surrender of the Germanic sound to a new eastern European sound, exotic, cheap and romantic. The march tune quickly turns into a waltz and passes into the hands of the violins who in turn have been corrupted. Their sound is lush and recalls the Strauss brothers. The scoring here is rich and openly comical and is always enormously enjoyed by the public. The more complex texture of Richard Strauss seems to enter the music and it ends firmly embedded in a dense sea of formalized romanticism.

The Finale makes no concessions. It opens on a long and complex discussion among the timpani, passing from intricate rhythmic playing to a violent frenzy of sound. Every conceivable percussive instrument seems involved and when the mightiest of the drums (the composer specifies Japanese drums for this task) end their battle the ground is cleared.

The brief fugal design of the rest of the Andante is sheer delight. The sound is purified and new. It does not accept the attempt of the violins to represent their old material and the formalized, icy dissonances turn into a music of burning intensity and controlled triumph. The ending is achieved emphatically and a series of Beethoven-like crashing chords end the movement, only they are gutted of their classical harmonies and the result is that the decisive chords imply a further sound – which never comes.

Eighth Symphony (1970)

The Eighth Symphony needs only a chamber orchestra. It is very close to Webern in its tonality and pared down orchestration. Yet the voice is distinctively König's and its fresh and radiant atmosphere is so inimitably his that you cannot hear the work without wanting to go on to his Ninth or Tenth where the closely cropped vine of the Eighth yields its rich wine.

The first movement displays the absolute command König has now achieved over his post-Webern sound. The strings directly announce the opening subject unchallenged and the pattern of sound is examined from every angle, reversed, transposed, dissected, the wind assist in the precise scrutiny of the theme and its potential. Once completed the small brass section present their summation, guided and controlled by muted horns.

The Second movement is a simple triple fugue worked out in the most meticulous detail, the genius lies in the scoring, in the lacunae, and in the unresolved phrasing, modern comment imposed on classical form.

The third movement is an audacious and totally successful reconstruction of a classical minuet and trio rendered up in gleaming modernity through König's elegant harmonics and the ravishing complexity of his scoring.

The end is intoxicating. A set of elusive phrases are rushed backwards and forwards among the four sections of the strings, weaving a more and more integrated sound. By the time the whole orchestra has entered into the design a tremendous task faces the conductor as each section seems to be pre-occupied with its own rhythms and tempi. The final phase is pure König. The material, far from being tied up is abruptly abandoned, a short new subject is introduced and quickly put in order by the strings and brass, each section participates and the conclusion is a triumphant flourish. The metaphors of intoxication are, on reflection, not accidental, but most appropriate to this most heady of symphonic delights.

Ninth Symphony (1973)

The Ninth Symphony which had its first performance in 1973 was given the title 'The German Symphony' by the composer. Architecturally it is König's vastest work in scope, length and means. An augmented orchestra is called for, the strings and brass are heavily reinforced, and there is a large choir with soloists as well as an organ. The concept is daunting. Its author's scheme is to present a survey of German music from Bach to Wagner heard through the medium of his own 'sound', the König sonority, as distinctive as that of any of his forebears. The miracle of the work is that it is never for a moment 'pastiche' of any of the styles reviewed in the symphony. It is neither pseudo-Bach nor mock Mozart. The König voice unifies and elevates the work so that it is his vision and assessment or summation of German music. It is a quest and a search as much as a tribute, as if König were seeking, in his abrupt key transitions, in his testing of different sets of harmonies, as he dissects for example the Wagnerian 'seamless web of music', to find what was their underlying truth. As if in the end he could arrive at some ultimate chord or harmonic pattern, a rhythmic curve that could encode the Germanic spirit.

There is no escaping the fact that this complicated and deep meditation on music is at the same time a philosophical examination and a moral statement. 'It is the thinking man's symphony,' wrote one critic after its first performance, 'and how moving it is!'

The first movement opens with the basic musical frame of the whole work which imposes its pattern on each individual structural element of this monumental symphony. This is in the contemporary König idiom, a canon, finely shaped, introduced by a flourish of brass and timpani then worked out through the string section. This yields to the first subject under examination. Using the slenderest of phrases by way of reference from Bach's Passacaglia in C Minor, B.W.V. 582, the organ embarks upon the kind of exploration that is the hallmark of the symphony. The organ's majestic Bachian fugal exercise enters into debate with the orchestra. The brass take over the 'voice' of Bachian expression leaving the organ free for König's complex musical observations, which far from being decorative extend the emotional field of the basic material.

The second movement takes audacity further as König with complete confidence of style takes a theme from the Adagio of Mozart's Dissonanzen Quartett K.V. 465, and the strings alone expand this in an exquisite tribute to his 'darling child'. It is as if König is unveiling to us a Mozart we did not know, the father of the modern idiom.

This leads us to the 'symphony within the symphony', a tiny Haydnesque jewel viewed through König's magic looking-glass. Again with only the most slender reference to the composer in question he sets off, this time with a phrase from the opening of Haydn's 'Die Jahreszeiten', and in choosing from one of the last works he reminds us that Haydn opened the way to his 'bad' pupil, Beethoven. The miniaturized symphony is a tour de force and although saturated in Haydn is still pure König. On the opening night and subsequently it has been customary to applaud the Inner Symphony on its completion, but it is a spontaneous response for no audience can sit silently and its sheer beauty demands recognition.

The fourth movement is the Beethoven. This is the most ambitious and difficult part of the work and here König emerges fully as an interpreter as well as guide through his own great tradition. König's musical reference is not to the symphonic works but to the Missa Solemnis. König presents his observation that the work is post-Christian, something which the Roman Catholic Church perceived in Beethoven's lifetime, for its place is not in a cathedral but a concert hall, and it has an almost official imprimatur on it. König's thesis is that since the composer rejected the crucifixion-redemption myth of meta-historical Christianity, it is more fitting for the Missa Solemnis to take on a text in accord with the revolutionary form of the music. König has selected texts from Nietzsche's private notebooks, posthumously named 'The Will to Power'. The shock and the force of these words in Beethovenian mode is devastating. Yet for the listener who has been following the argument from the beginning of the symphony it is musically and philosophically inevitable. The uncomfortable fact is that everybody on hearing it knows perfectly well that Beethoven would have preferred Nietzsche to the ritual tale of the crucifixion myth.

The tenor opens with the declaration: 'Life is only a MEANS to something – it is the expression of forms of the growth of power.' (W.P. 706) The glorious scoring of the 'Sanctus' sustains the choral statement: 'Value is the highest quantum of power that a man is able to incorporate – a man! not mankind. Mankind is ever a means rather than an end. It is a question of the result. Mankind is merely the experimental material, the tremendous surplus of failures – a field of ruins.' (W.P. 713) The triumphant Nietzschean 'resurrection' of the New Man is built around the aphorism: 'Value words are banners raised – where a NEW BLISS has been found, a new feeling!'

The author of the new feeling was of course, Wagner, Nietzsche's beloved enemy. The finale of the symphony is the more extraordinary for coming after the tumultuous energy of the exultant celebration of the Overman. It is healing and serene. It is the Wagner of affirmation of the gift by woman to man, which is spoken of in the Siegfried Idyll, the reflective passages between Wotan and Brünnhilde and the core of Die Meistersinger. Here there is not one single Wagner chord, König's scoring is immaculate, and yet one is unmistakably in the realm of the master of Bayreuth. The solo soprano voice enhances this tribute to women and to the modern defender of women, Richard

Wagner, the last and the greatest of the giants of German music.

As the Wagnerian essay closes there is a recapitulation of the opening thematic material that has been constantly present, and in a muted serene passage of great beauty it closes this mighty symphonic tribute to the German spirit.

Tenth Symphony (1975)

If König's Ninth is his monument to the past, the Tenth is his message for the future. To produce three great masterpieces in six years is itself phenomenal, but what is astonishing is the sheer range of König's genius. He struggled to assimilate his own and Germany's past, consciously and under fire, in order to confirm his deep conviction that the future of the world needed its spiritual and philosophical energy to reach a new stage in man's story.

From the Fifth Symphony one can trace a quite logical and demonstrable development of his musical language. At the same time and despite the architectural complexity of the Ninth it is possible to identify a constant return to the Webernian principle of 'intensity by minimal means' as well as an obsession with certain intellectual issues. Yet in the Tenth one has to acknowledge a quantum leap to a quite new language. Just as no one could have foretold the capacity of music to handle the Wotan-Fricka or the Wotan-Brünnhilde duologues from listening to Wagner's immediate predecessors, so it is difficult to realize that music could deal with the intractably intellectual formulae of the Tenth from listening to the superficiality of the rest of contemporary music.

The Tenth Symphony rather than being an argument or a working-out in the Beethoven sense, is a definition, a theorem, or even a matrix. It consists of pure musical and linguistic patterns, that is, terms, phrases and statements along with their musical equivalents. The verbal language is abstruse and at times incomprehensible, equally, the musical method is unnervingly new, unlike anything before it. It is as if on the one hand the composer had recovered something of the Baroque sense of music as mathematics and wedded it to Wagner's perception that music could convey states of consciousness, then to this he has added his own unique contribution by which musically structured text could implant a philosophy deep into the listener's being.

The Tenth is not a choral symphony in the sense

that his Ninth is. Here the text is sung by choir and soloists in such a manner that the human voices function as another section of the orchestra. One could say that König has created the first choral symphony, and from this point of view Beethoven's Ninth and the choral Mahlers are more like cantatas. The genius of Beethoven was that his music expressed the equivalent of the Schiller text – there is no doubt that the music 'conveys' what the words declare. The achievement of König is that he transmits a philosophy, an ontology and its experience in musical language – using words.

The Symphony is divided into four sections which have headings to indicate their main subjects. The whole work is a description of the human self on its quest for knowledge of itself and existence, and the stages of this journey. The text is taken from Johann König's 'Nietzsche Dialogues', and his still unpublished 'The Now'. Despite the title of the former work its thesis is not Nietzschean but an attempt, as the author puts it, to present 'a post-Nietzschean view for the modern world that emerged after the destruction of Germany by the internationalists.' It employs the difficult vocabulary and usage of ontological enquiry.

The first section is entitled: Geworfenheit. Das Mann.

The second: Das Nichts. Tod.
The third: Jetzt. Hellsichtig.
The fourth: Das Heitere.

In the opening section man is described as being thrown into existence, into immediate self-confrontation without any knowledge except glimmerings of false information. He becomes lost in the world as it is, submerged and overwhelmed until his own self-awareness transforms into a feeling absorbed by the They, he is in danger of becoming a Not, or Nothing. This is the theme of the second section. There is a sense of crisis and loss, the earlier triviality and curiosity is transformed into urgent and desperate need to confront one's own death. Having felt homeless and without meaning, in the third section man comes to accept finitude and mortality and in doing so a meaningful experience of the present and the Now revitalizes his being. The fruit of this is the moment of clear vision which brings with it Light, and with the Light comes knowing joy, 'die wissende Heiterkeit'.

The four sections are played through without a break. The scoring is ruthlessly symmetrical on the page like Bach and there is no sweep or drift of sound, but rather a totally structured onslaught of music whose sonority makes impact by its unpredictability and absence of a fixed tonal centre. Unlike the Ninth, there is only an augmented chamber orchestra, restricted and balanced. The choir is small and the four soloists, tenor, bass, soprano and contralto, are employed almost without ceasing throughout the symphony.

The intricate relationship of voices to instruments ensures that much of the text is not assimilated as text but only as sound, but those sections where suddenly a solo voice illuminates the music are very particularly selected to make maximum impact.

The emotional scope is remarkable, from the turbulent and violent opening, through a growing tension and angst that leads to a ferocious and explosive climax. Beyond this opens out a bleak and tormenting wasteland where words and sound thin out almost to silence. This struggles fitfully to life and a new excitement enters so that each moment is an urgent and over-vivid separate experience. From this the condition clarifies, becomes more confident, fuller, until a full free-floating energy is transformed into one blinding moment of vision – an unforgettable moment of total sound from the choir and orchestra – then the rich satisfying and complex profundity of the deeply radiant 'knowing joy' of the dedication.

As the Berlin music critic wrote of this work after its premiere, 'With his Tenth Symphony König took us to the limit and then in the last movement he crossed the line.'

Chapter Three

König's World of Ideas

The foundation of Gorka König's world-view lies in his youthful experience of Germany and Europe in the late 1930s. We would distinguish three dynamic elements in his intellectual life: monetary reform doctrines ending in a categoric opposition to usury and the current monetary system as being a cause of world slavery; the concept that the psyche itself forms the basis of any politique and thus the need to create the New Man, an ontological view which posits total freedom of possibilities for man whose role is to dominate the cosmos; and Being itself which is unconditioned and unique. It is as a musician that he unites and draws together these three sciences, politics, psychology and philosophy.

It is ironic that the simplest element in the equation is the one that is transformed into the most difficult, and this is a sign of how much irrationality and naked politics and prejudice circle around the theme. König's destiny was to be born a German who spent his formative years in the ambience of the Third Reich. He was received with honour by the state and was privileged, for that was the contemporary view, with a private and intimate access to the Führer. These meetings took place when he was around nineteen years of age. He has never wavered in his mature years either from his confirmation that at the time he was enormously moved and exalted by these meetings, or from his refusal to denounce or reject his own experience. König on the subject is crystal clear, he has had every opportunity to define his position for he has been persecuted, plagued and humiliated by vicious attacks from people who have implied that his denunciation of Hitler and the Nazis was some kind of price that was non-negotiable and had to be paid before he could be admitted to the halls of fame.

There is no doubt that König had a clearly defined position on naziism and it was neither pro nor anti, and the ferocious insistence that this was not good enough was to him the clearest indicator of just how powerful the dominant dialectic of the new society was. Sometimes to clarify his position he would make several propositions at once, to try by paradox and inversion to cut through the blind fanaticism of the new 'humanism'.

He said: 'Hitler was a roman catholic who was never ex-communicated.' He said: 'The swastika is a cross, perhaps it was the last Christian crusade against the invader from the east.' He said: 'The swastika is a broken cross, for it smashed Christian culture and exposed both the ancient culture before its defeat and the new barbarism after the enemies' victory. The Wehrmacht fought the last crusade, and after them came the horrific power of an elite which had created nuclear weapons.' He said: 'Hitler was deceived. He only understood power politics and war. He had studied the Ring but understood too late that this was precisely the scenario of his enemies. Like Siegfried he was naif. His own Christian culture was at last destroyed, and by his hand. It was over. Now the whole thing has begun again with new gods in Valhalla, new dwarfs and new giants. The enemy have the Ring, the Spear and the Tarnhelm – that is the Usury-cycle (inflation-deflation), the Nuclear Weapon, and the Mask of Politics which hides the monetary elite, making them invisible.'

He also said: 'Why do you want him as a devil? History is not like that. He was a man. Why must everything surrounding him be unspeakable, unnamable, and fraught with a vocabulary of hysteria and insult? There are no, I repeat, no villains in history, and no holy martyrs, even in their millions. There is no sacred arithmetic of suffering.'

His last word on the subject was: 'My war statistic is that over thirty million people were destroyed in order that usury would not be abolished, but would triumph over the whole world after the defeat of Germany until every nation was in the throes of an intolerable spiral of debt and the power elite ruled by supranationalist decree.' He said that in 1950.

His 'Yesterday's victims are tomorrow's executioners' had him condemned as a fascist, but he stubbornly refused the title, to the scorn of his enemies and the chagrin of those romantic enough to think they could recapture the past. His final understanding of these dramatic years of his youth was to be redefined later in his philosophic and psychological re-appraisal as it emerged in the years with his wife and his father. He was an unrepentant Nietzschean and at least he lived to see the greatest modern philosopher re-valued to some extent in the late 1960s, but even there he resented the condescension of the inarticulate in grudgingly admitting the undeniable genius of the Saxony master.

Nothing infuriated his enemies more than his refusal to be drawn into the debate of his contemporaries. It was all irrelevant, he insisted. He rejected the right-left dialectic, the pro-anti racism dialectic, his basic conviction was that the crucial issue of the age was being deliberately obscured and it was neither a conspiracy nor ignorance. The only vital moral issue for the survival of, rather the recreation of, civilization was the abolition of usury, which implied a complete dismantling of the monetary system created in the wake of the Second World War.

His brief experience in the Third Reich followed by his exile in Switzerland and his exposure to Slav expatriates added a complexity and texture to his thinking on power politics. As a result he found it impossible to believe in the official version of history. His Yugoslavian friends had convinced him that it was ridiculous to claim that the First World War was started because of the assassination of the heir to the throne of the Austro-Hungarian Empire, and they insisted that the Black Hand, as indeed other European secret societies, far from being a nationalist freedom movement, was part of a wider plan for the destruction of the old order, the 'Christendom of nineteenth-century Europe'. Puric, who had been significantly in place in London near to Churchill during part of the war, had further insisted that the key to understanding the twentieth century lay in the disparity of conditions before and after the two major conflicts. The 'purpose' of each war and its actual result were clear evidence of a most powerful policy which was never openly displayed until executed.

Hitler, claimed König, had explained that the First World War could only be understood by an examination of what happened on the eastern front of Germany and had warned him to watch how the destiny of civilization lay in what would happen again on the eastern front. König interpreted this to mean that the outcome of the first conflict was the establishment of communism in Russia and its infiltration into eastern Europe and Germany, and the result of the second had turned out to be the establishment of communist hegemony over half of the German Reich. Puric had said: 'They are the victors, they are allies. They can do what they want, and look what they want! War was declared in order to fulfil a treaty obligation to defend Poland in the event of attack. Millions are killed as a result of this policy and at the end Poland is handed over to soviet communism! It does not make sense, nor do their alibis. From the beginning another programme was being carried out.'

König also reported Hitler's bafflement at the British desire to 'go to war over Poland' saying, 'If they lose the war they have lost the empire, if they win the war they will have lost the empire by exhaustion of means. It does not make sense!' Puric had confirmed this politique, while a deadly enemy of the Nazis! His understanding was, 'This is, in a very real sense, Churchill's war. The way was cleared for him. The British parliamentary system was utterly corrupted and it was not difficult to manoeuvre the war party into place. The first stage had been the removal of the king in England. Churchill had fought this at first but then he had to give in, as a debtor he was already in the hands of the enemy before 1939, for they had saved him from bankruptcy and disgrace. Hitler cannot win because he is fighting a power politics scenario and the enemy are not. They have a no-lose scenario because if you can compel your enemy to fight by one limited set of rules, while you play by another freer set of rules you must win. They are on the right and the left. The Christian monarchies and value system of that epoch have been destroyed. The old politics are irrelevant.' This was Puric's argument. König differed from Puric and the rightists he knew in that he did not wish to 'return' to a previous set of values.

The important new element in König's thinking which categorically separates him from rightist thinking is his philosophical background which permitted him to make a radical re-appraisal of politics. His view was Nietzschean, but still except to an elite this implies a right-wing 'superman' ideology. Of course, this was never Nietzsche's view, and the Übermensch is a much deeper concept. It is a sign of the unity of König's thought that as we try to examine the foundations of his view and touch on the political we are involved in the psychological and the philosophical. König, following his father's analysis, accepted the five point view of Nietzsche as being:

1. Nihilism
2. Re-valuation of all previous values
3. The will to power
4. The eternal recurrence of the same
5. The Overman

We will return to this matrix. Just now it is enough to comment on its application by König in the contemporary context. He saw the disgrace of the Weimar Republic as confirming and bringing about an absolute rejection of 'Christian sentiment and weakness' in the Nietzschean assessment, thus leading to a creative nihilism. This force, once released, during its rise confronted the subversive elements at work in Europe. König points out the original goal of National Socialism was noble but they later became distracted through entering into alliance with the monetarist forces in order to build their war machine, unaware that 'foreign banking' was not different from 'national banking'. That original, noble aim had been clearly defined in the 1920 'Proclamation of the 25 Points' as being liberation from 'the bondage of interest'.

The revaluation of all previous values had come in the ferocious and relentless determination to create a post-Christian technological society. Thus the ideology had to speak of a new force in place of the corrupt 'humanism' of the disgusting Weimar epoch and its terrible economic anarchy. The will to power exerted itself but having its own inexorable logic in it working out on the forces involved it produced results that were not foreseen by any party in the process. And here König is clearly not a conspirationalist or revisionist. He saw it as fitting that Hitler did what he did but accepts the outcome – firstly, the saving of the German state from anarchy and degradation, secondly the confirmation of a true and ancient Germanic tradition in culture and knowledge. Thirdly came the confrontation with the demons of the age, as Puric called them, those forces of insurrection and revolution which had been dismantling the fabric of western society since the French Revolution and with the same Jacobin ideology. Thus König sees history without emotional prejudice. He sees as inevitable the 'release' of power of new forces in society precisely because they were suppressed and persecuted. The force of Nazi power releases the nuclear weaponry in the West. The morally self-righteous victims become forced by the 'eternal recurrence of the same' to re-enact an identical scenario of will to power in the Arab world, only now as executioners with a new slave class to disinherit.

In this viewpoint König sees all humanity 'in the same boat', and his examination therefore does not stop at a scenario of good versus evil, but rather goes on to demand what are the root issues and factors of the disease of civilization and how can the will to power activate itself in order to give man domination in the world and yet not destroy the ground of existence, the world itself. In that sense he approves the creation of nuclear weaponry held, as he understands it, by one political hegemony. The danger is not war but man himself for unless the Overman does emerge man would rather commit 'suicide', that is nuclear holocaust, than lose power and wealth.

Here mention should be made of König's deep reading of the Ring, and his view of Wagner as a true revolutionary, and this again impinges on the psychology of men and women and the Overman doctrine. It is in his reading of the Ring that the influence of Pound is most clear. There is no doubt that the conversations with Pound made a tremendous impact on the composer and from him he understood for the first time that it was usury itself that was the destructive force that had to be eradicated from modern society if the civilization of Europe was to be liberated and not just remain as a skeletal political structure and a spiritual corpse.

He saw all ecological issues, and all issues of nuclear war, and the armament industry as subsumed under the workings-out of the usury economy. His sponsorship of a return to a bi-metal currency, gold and silver, and the abolition of paper (worthless promissory note) money as well as the stock market (a criminal usury mechanism) and the futures market were so radically ahead of their time that he met with little comprehension. The issue was simple but the official doctrine was so brilliantly imposed on the masses that it could not be understood. At this time, with the demonstrable irrationality of the monetary system, 'getting to the root of the malaise' is easier. In the 1950s and 1960s the subject was considered arcane, now it is urgent. One cannot be anti-nuclear, was König's argument, unless one is anti-usury.

His position was that the whole apparatus of political debate is itself a brilliantly designed trap to canalize and impotize the masses who believe in the myths of nationalism, allowing the power elite to maintain their elusive force by being supra-national and at the same time maintaining a 'national entity' in permanent crisis to divert attention from the actual power operation achieved entirely through manipulation of the monetary cycle, or, as he liked to call it, the Ring.

Modern 'terrorism' he saw as the impotent and desperate means of the new oppressed to get a justice that not only eludes them but clearly cannot in terms of the power structure ever be achieved. He opposed it as a doctrine of ignorance, and insisted that the power of the dominant regime was the money-system itself. Just as Pound was declared insane for finding out the truth, and accused of fascism to make him 'unacceptable' to intellectuals, so König too was dismissed as a Nazi with 'eccentric' monetarist theories from the 1930s.

König shared with Pound a difficult burden to bear, people loved him but when he presented his theories they resented or hated him, not because they could not understand him but because they could, and felt helpless or lacked the will to alter the injustice of the time. This is what over the years drove König out of the realm of anti-usury politics, although he never changed position on this issue, into the world of philosophy and the psychology of the Overman.

In his psychological orientation it is not surprising that the primary influence is his gifted wife, Frieda Ludendorff. From the time of their first meeting she was a determined anti-Freudian. She saw that Freud had lifted all that had weight in his theories from Nietzsche and simply stood it on its head, or genitals, as she preferred to say, just as Marx had merely reversed the already systematized world-view of Hegel. Her work, later much influenced by Johann König, had been to relocate psychiatric and psychological assessment in the mainstream of German philosophy, even, she once said, 'in a post-Kantian frame'. The profound reason for her rejection of Freud was in its placing of the analyst in a position of unassailability and fantasy separateness from the suffering subject, while at the same time robbing the patient of his existential freedom with the doctrine of the Unconscious which implied that an inaccessible source of power controlled the self which the self did not have knowledge of, thus losing integral freedom. The Unconscious implies the lack of responsibility for actions and therefore of will. The Being of a person is will to power and this policy cuts off the subject from access to his own force. Politically, therefore, it is a methodology designed to set up subservient masses. Anxiety, from being an impulse to approach one's own Being becomes translated into an impulse to destruction or paralysis. Thus a treatment implies a removal of the natural impulse of the psyche to find its new equilibrium in a transvaluation of old values (tyranny of parents, living for others) and denies the struggling self its will to power. The analyst is himself exerting absolute power over the patient and establishing himself as part of a new elite with the patient as the working or slave class. The work of the patient is to be 'ill' for the psychiatrist, and his slavery is to be rehabilitated within his frozen neurosis as a dutiful and grateful as well as tranquillized consumer in the usury economy. The obligatory payment before each session of analysis is the usurious transaction that enslaves the patient and ensconces the doctor in his role as banker. With that transaction he takes the patient's will to power and reduces him to poverty and the doctor to wealth. In this system the patient needs the doctor as the debtor needs the bank to go on being in debt. The necessary point in the analysis when the patient 'revolts' against the analyst, and expresses openly his hostility, is cunningly transformed into its opposite, the identification which marks the mid-point in the control system. Once the patient has projected his fixation onto the doctor it only remains for the doctor to return it to the patient as his own 'authenticity', and his new self is one that has acquiesced in the psycho-analytical process so that, far from being liberated, the patient carries in his gut the same anguish only now it does not hurt – thus he will never be free, and he will never discover the ground of his own being.

That in crude summation is the Ludendorff position on the Freudian tradition – indeed on the whole idea of 'therapy'. Set over and against this negative review is her vital and constructive position in seeing illness as a means to passing beyond the previous existential condition. It is here that one can see in action, and it is most intriguing, the synergistic effect of the three Königs on each other, for there is no doubt that in the last years of Johann König, the three of them shared a remarkably dynamic and unified intellectual experience.

Frieda Ludendorff's main contribution to psychiatric practice lies in her work with autistic children and to its theory in her presenting in a clinical context the philosophical concepts of Johann König. Essentially, Ludendorff proposes that instead of building a clinical picture of the human psyche on a basis of studying in Gide's famous phrase 'infants and invalids', an attempt should be made to examine man in his highest manifestations, and it is her proposal that psychiatric method should constructively design the new man, and correct the faults in the formational process to create a type of being who functions on a more rational and powerful drive system.

Frieda Ludendorff's contribution to König is her proposition that the politique is the product of the will to power of the self on its journey to the Overman and therefore negatively or positively the urge to arrive at 'a better matrix' will produce the neuroses or psychoses in the individual as well as the social setting for them. The Keynesian economic doctrine is a direct result of the Keynesian neurosis fitting the needs of the dominant group. Marx's alienation transforms itself into politics in his own exorcism of his unfulfilled aggressive drives. It is not for one moment that the personality creates the politique, but rather that the historical process responds to the higher individual who can express a key neurosis in a manner that fits the mode of the historical moment. If the historical moment will not receive the signal, does not recognize the sign, then a normal psychosis results. 'I am Napoleon!' in the madhouse. If the man makes the signals and the people respond there is an army and a government to obey his command. The reason for the trapped pattern of history, 'learning from the mistakes of the past to make the mistakes of the future', is that the individual's drive towards will to power is motivated by desperation and psychic need, rather than by plenitude of being and conscious choice which is the Overman.

If Ludendorff stopped there her theory would be no more than intriguing. Where she becomes interesting is in her analysis of what the formative matrices are on which the active psyche is built. She reads the psychic subject backwards as it were, to observe where the drives to historicity come from, and in doing this she indicates how the eternal recurrence of the same in most people is cyclical biology and inherited characteristics.

She sees in Brünnhilde not a romantic destroying herself because she has lost her lover, but a new being who enters the arena of politics because only she has understood the duplicity of 'history' and seen through it. The failure of her husband to do so had cost him his life. The Cycle ends because she divines that all the ills have come not from her or from Siegfried but from the motive force of everybody's actions throughout the whole saga which is the unbridled quest for the Ring, which means power, and that power in turn puts the access to gold under their hand. She demonstrates that there is a higher will to power than the will to power gained by possession of the Ring, and that is the unselfish desire – born of man-woman love (not Christian sentiment) – to restore things to their basic natural balance, that is, the destruction of the fantasy arena of power politics, Valhalla, and of the false Overmen, and the unjust enslavement of the masses, and most radically, the elimination of the power elite and their secret infighting which is hidden from the masses. So it is that Brünnhilde's act is not self-immolation but maximum will to power to destroy the old order inspired by pure and constructive nihilism, opening the way to a completely new transvaluation of values through the possibility of an eternal recurrence which is the necessary result of the return to primal harmony. In that model both Siegfried and Brünnhilde are Overmen who clear the path for the next cycle of existence.

In this model Ludendorff looks to the formation of the basic personality and finds its short-circuiting lies in the unconscious repetition of the infantile 'play' in the theatrical sense. 'Naughty! Naughty!' calls out the child to the doll, beginning the pattern of re-enactment. Education, according to her, lies in de-programming the expected response, in redefining the decided definition of the authoritative other, in opening up the awareness of possibilities in growth, and in recognizing the high-drive child early on in order to begin the conscious preparation of an elite. 'The education of the best for the safety of the rest' and in order that 'history should happen'. It is the fear of the masses that history will happen which has placed the world in jeopardy. Brazenly ignorant politicians tell the masses that 'thanks to nuclear weapons' nothing has happened, when in fact they have made everything happen and it is all bad getting worse.

Ludendorff has in her clinical study of autistic children suggested that they are the historical product, by definition, of the democratic process. In order to be fully accepted and safe you avoid the spontaneous totally and decide only to repeat what the previous signal is – that is what democracy is in its nature. The majority must be right, so do not deviate from their signal. Fortunes are spent on the malformed, and the malfunctioning and the brain-damaged not out of 'compassion' but to ensure that people do not look up to the superior but are held in the thrall of false 'pity' for the inferior, thus ensuring the continued tyranny of the usurious elite. Wisdom can only return as will to power, and will to power cannot be made without the desire for the Overman. The Overman cannot be created ideologically but only by education which is formative and de-programming. The new man would be the child of an erotically loving 'brother and sister' – Siegmund and Sieglinde – in the myth, and thus also an orphan so that the higher self comes from inside out and not imposed from a historical precedent. This was Frieda Ludendorff's radical and controversial contribution to her age and to her husband's thought.

König's philosophical position is inevitably some quintessential response to his father's post-Nietzschean ontology. It provides the summit of his thinking whose foundations lay in his own youthful experience.

In the same way that König seems to encapsulate his historical tradition inside his own development, his father represents a lifetime's assimilation of the German idealist school culminating in the 'final' position of Nietzsche, who in his turn had come as a summing-up of all before him, and in the opening of a new philosophical discourse. It is worth recalling that Johann König began his intellectual life as a neo-Kantian of the Baden School. So he emerged with a mind trained in the classical method of the Greeks as negotiated through the post-Kantians. Fichte and Hegel, the experimental psychologist Hugo Munsterberg and, of course, Husserl brought him into the contemporary debate. He always maintained a deep personal attachment to Kant the man as well as the thinker and on his deathbed he smiled up at his son and quoted to him the dying words of the Königsberg philosopher, 'Es ist gut!' And he used to say in his last years, 'From Königsberg to König is only a step.'

Rickert and Husserl led him inevitably into the method of ontological thinking. He had no difficulty with the concept that the phenomenological and not the scientific method gives access to man's way of being. It was step by step that he moved to his own position, 'Following the alpine guide across the rapids of existential thought.' It was inevitable that the thinker of Freiburg would find Nietzsche inescapable. He saw that Nietzsche study had wasted so much time dithering between two critical positions, one that he was not a systematic but an aphoristic philosopher, the other that he was a systematic philosopher and his system had been applied socially and had proved to be abominable. The first view held a semantic problem and the second a political one. König's contribution was that he approached Nietzsche opening himself to his message and its profundity without raising any barriers of prejudice or pre-conception. He considered the ambiguity of Nietzsche to Wagner was of the richest value for serious students of the age. He worked out with Frieda Ludendorff a fascinating study of the relationship between Nietzsche's personal attachment to Richard and Cosima Wagner, as a couple and as individuals, and the ideological recognition and rejection of Wagner's work. Despite the ambiguity and vehemence of many of Nietzsche's statements, they basically agreed that Wagner was a great revolutionary thinker up until the problem of Parsifal. Like Nietzsche, they could not escape the impact of Wagner's art and vision, and were as engaged with him in their own way as Nietzsche was and never ceased to be.

Johann König's work is the series of Socratic Dialogues conducted in an imaginary lunatic asylum between König and Nietzsche, or is it a real one in which König is talking to himself? This fundamental uncertainty about the ground of one's own being is the subject examined again and again by the two (one) in the discussion. Nietzsche is measured against the early Greeks, Plato ('the great viaduct of corruption') and the trap of morality are examined, Descartes in his role of precursor of Nietzsche and as his enemy. König with his psychological insights honed by Ludendorff is quick to spot the pattern of passionate and dialectically dazzling negation of the 'loved ones', God, of course, and Plato,

Descartes, and Wagner, subjects he was infinitely better on than those from which he maintained a respectful distance, Aristotle, Goethe.

His existentialism in the end is his psychological doctrine. Despite his defining himself in that dialectic, he is in all his later writings deeply engaged in the question of Being and in the Nietzschean theme of the embodiment of the Overman and in the political confrontation of the disaster of democracy which has enslaved the world, preaching humanism while devaluing the human being. König insisted a metaphysical appraisal had to precede a political initiative. He, like Gorka, was not a romantic, and his relationship to the National Socialists was at its strongest before they fell into the trap the internationalists set for them. In the end, embedded in the ontological texture of thinking that he had lived over the years, he turned to the theme of political responsibility, not in the quotidian dialectics that Sartre engaged in which trivialized his thinking, but in a deeply reflected vision of what kind of state had to be produced to serve a modern society.

In his Nietzschean-Platonic Republic König returns to the urgent cultural imperative of forming again an elite leadership trained in the highest philosophical discipline and grounded in a new form of self-awareness. The Overman, he insists, cannot be avoided – it is one of the key concepts of the modern world.

It would be safe to say that Johann König laid down the philosophical ground on which both Frieda with her concepts of the whole psyche and Gorka with his vision of an integrated worldview were able to build their creative works. König's music is overtly philosophical, and frankly involves the listener in a world of ideas and vision which is itself political. In his extension of the capacity of musical expression he follows the great German tradition which he deliberately and insistently acknowledges. All he is doing is extending the intellectual territory gained by Bach, Mozart, Beethoven and Wagner, each said 'more' than the former, went further. With the crowning achievement of his Tenth Symphony König makes us enter a realm until now closed to us. There can be no denying the enormous intellectual influence that König's music has wrought in the realm of ideas. People who respond to his music respond to his thought and reach out for his world of ideas after they have entered into his world of music.

People unacquainted with the philosophical discourse in which Nietzsche made his infamous pronouncements excoriating the repellent decadence of Christian morals and sentiments, jubilantly confirming nihilism and atheism, climaxed by the notorious 'God is dead!', and the rejection of herd-man in preference for the Overman crudely renamed in translations as the Superman – and regrettably some people who should know better and have even read Nietzsche after some technical training in metaphysics – found in the König family's passionate involvement in his writings a proof of some eccentricity of thought which put them outside the mainstream of contemporary thinking. This was hardly convincing, for there was regrettably no mainstream of contemporary thinking in progress, philosophical discourse had been halted placing philosophy alongside archaeology or not even that since its exponents had also stopped digging.

This forces us to examine a theme which König the composer spoke of often, that is, a creative artist like a musician, and his work, are not two separate entities but two inter-related creations. The life and the work cannot be separated. König even saw the financial struggle of Beethoven as part of the heroic element in his music. Beethoven and Wagner both tried to create a world in which the humiliation of the corrupt monetary system was vanquished, and both struggled heroically not just for their worldview but to survive economically. Mozart was killed by it, being too weak and too young to struggle. His act of becoming a freemason was his tactic to evade economic disaster, he paid the usurers his dues, but he was unable to collect.

König's thought is enlaced irrevocably with his musical statements. But it must not be considered through ignorance or through out-dated or propagandist readings of Nietzsche, or through some denigration of the great German tradition in idealist thought, that the nihilism of Nietzsche is a zero position so to speak, that his atheism is a denial of Being as such, that his loathing of Christian compassion is inhuman but rather, in the end it is not more utopianism, but a confirmation of life. It is tragic that one has to defend this great genius of the European spirit but otherwise it is impossible to defend König, father and son.

It was Nietzsche who declared, 'No! God the Supreme Power – that's enough! Everything follows from it, 'the world' follows from it.' König the philosopher saw in Nietzsche the supreme metaphysicist and agreed with that view which said that in the deepest sense he had brought the metaphysical discourse to an end, or rather he had brought discourse to an end. There was no way the eternal recurrence of the same could emerge until the complete transvaluation of values had taken place, and that meant the rejection of the unscientific thinking of Christian theology which does not permit philosophical discourse since redemptionist intervention short-circuits any need for it. What emerged in the Königian view was that after necessary and creative nihilism had been affirmed this opened the way to a pure ontology and a new way of seeing the potential of man, and thus, by implication the opportunity to posit a new society.

König insisted that the confirmation of Being had to be encased in a double negative, one absolute and one conditional, and directive – showing the lines along which one could speak and the lines along which one could not speak without repeating the dead dialogue of the old religion. As Being was freed by its protected definition, a definition which allowed one to speak of man's being there and Being itself, the vision of the Overman began to present itself, the Overman of Being, the free spirit, the orphan-leader, the New Man. This intellectual event was by definition a political scenario, and it was one which exalted an elite, for only from an elite could emerge the elect of the elite and only from the elect could emerge the Overman. The Overman's doctrine implied war, not nuclear suicidal war which was a crime against humanity, but a noble war without which man could not reach his highest condition. The Nietzschean wildness, the Dionysiac power that he celebrated, could not be crushed, for that would mean a return to the nothing-happening fear psychology of the Judaeo-Christian slave mentality. As Nietzsche put it: 'Paradise lies under the shadow of the swords! Also a symbol and slogan by which beings of noble and warlike origin reveal themselves and recognise each other.'

There is no avoiding this element in König the composer's thought, and in it he found himself in harmony with both his wife and his father. This conviction, it must not be forgotten, comes from a man who had declared that the creators and developers of nuclear weapons were the greatest criminals in the history of mankind and that those who design them and govern under them were criminals and should be tried by international court under the same rules and methods employed at Nuremberg, accusing them of crimes against humanity, and worse, the crime of intending the destruction of the human species itself, an all-racial holocaust, which would bring about the end of mankind and the planet. Yet even in this dialectic König was convinced that the key lay in the abolition of the usury, for the new power elite were nuclear usurists, they used nuclear weaponry to create fear and in its shadow used monetarist magic to create world enslavement and debt.

Thus it was that König's world-view was a unified whole and it always led back to the metaphysical meditation on which it was founded and without which he was convinced no constructive politique of the future could be forged, or rather no possible future could be forged. The will to power had to force the hand of the nuclear usurists who would rather be immolated than give up the Ring. This time it had to happen without taking the ground from under the feet of the human race. There had to be a Rhine to receive the gold again, there had to be the people to turn serenely triumphant from the destruction of the old values. This, said König, was the struggle of the age. If the victory of Nietzsche had been the death of religion, the victory the Königs wanted was the death of politics, which masked the usurious process that enslaved mankind. It was to this end that his symphonies from the Seventh onwards had been written, and if one looked carefully one could discern that it had been his concern right from the very beginning when he took those solitary walks in the Black Forest and the Bavarian Alps with Adolf Hitler.

Gorka König was a child of his time. He became a man. Attention must be paid to this man, for he speaks of life and of survival, as the great Ring Cycle once again comes to its completion.

Chapter Four
König's World of Music

In the work of Gorka König there are two elements that attract attention. One is the actual language of his musical development and expression and the other is his intellectual conviction that music is not merely expressive in the sense of conveying feelings but can handle ideational material, even concepts transmitted in a manner particular to music. König insists that music is itself a language but not the same as grammatical language. He has gone as far as to say that there are different layers of language which the human brain can communicate with: the lowest language level is visual sign language. This is the language of politics and therefore psychology. It is the language of signs, symbols, gestures, recognition and rejection. It is the language of basic sanity and confirmation of the other as having its own reality along with oneself. Total absence of signal is a clinical evidence of insanity.

It is the high language of sexuality, touch being a sub-language but the low or fundamental means of sexual communication. Its highest linguistic expression is dance.

Verbal language is the basic form of communication. It contains several layers of contact. The basic sign being merely an extension of sight-language with verbal indicators, this is used in ordinary life exchanges. This complexifies into information exchange, now the dominant social mode of communication. Above that is poetry which is not based on logically structured units of information like concepts and propositions, but is based on the abstract entity which can 'interpret' the metaphor from its example to its meaning. The capacity to 'read' meaning into metaphor is the border-line of being human, it is a transformative faculty which allows some world of inner reality to translate itself into a new apprehension of outer existence. It is the metaphysical 'edge' of consciousness and communication.

The third and highest layer of communication is music, not all music. Just as touch ends when one hand separates from the other and one must look to see, so music passes from its own low stage to higher levels. All primitive and folk music allied to the dance is the low level, this is rhythm based and so tied to sexuality. Yet even rhythm itself could be structured and paced to make another kind of communication possible. This was still not the high language of German music, now called western music. Its discovery was sonority, sound texture. Firstly in a mathematical set of patterns which produced harmonics of varied resonance. This reached an astonishingly sophisticated stage very early in its history. Baroque music as it is deceptively called began to reveal unexpected and far-reaching capacities of communication. A recent application of Baroque adagios as an aid to memorization proved to be verifiably successful because of a particular brain-wave the sound produced which collaborated in the learning process. That, of course, was side-effect, but not insignificant. By the time of Bach, German music had been called upon to express or describe highly complex mathematical patterns of aural exchange; canon, fugue, reversal, and transposition of key opened up the music to convey states of human emotion in describing suffering, death, and a spiritual exaltation of a transcendent nature. It was, in its religious role, taking man into a particular realm of both feelings and ideas. The ideas were carried by the religious framework of masses and passion-plays. Yet in this a discovery if not made was acted upon, and that was that certain states could be induced, which while they were emotional contained in them an intellectual series of references to belief and the higher self. As we will see a transposition of the musical language later proved that the music could 'speak for itself'.

Music in its early phase divided itself in its higher reaches, according to the Christian culture in which it grew, into two, sacred and profane. The profane music often was carried in a classical re-counting of love fables, like Dido and Aeneas. Here the same discovery was made that subtle states of erotic longing and human contact could be conveyed in that same manner which in poetry sets up a communication which is different from prose (which as Molière pointed out the bourgeois has been speaking without even knowing) yet not much serious attention was paid to this growing capacity of music to communicate across a broader and broader spectrum. Music, despite the church was still, also, delicious entertainment.

In 1740 the Mannheim composers began to express pure musical structures of a new complexity. The symphony was being born. In 1756 Johann Wenzel Stamitz wrote over seventy symphonies for an orchestra comprising thirty strings, four horns, two flutes as well as oboes, clarinets, bassoons, trumpets, and timpani. The Berlin school and the Viennese school spread the popularity of the form. In 1773 C. P. E. Bach was commissioned to write six symphonies. With Haydn and Mozart the form took enormous strides in both style and content. Alongside the symphony came the unique phenomenon of Mozart, König's 'darling child', who brought to opera his own private world of ravishing infantile sexuality projected onto the stage with a startling array of dramatic characters expressing various forms of erotic longing and ambition. Aristocrats and servants and mythic figures all held in a musical thrall of eternal desire, again without the public really grasping what had happened at the time, created a new dimension for his musical genius to unfold in the human heart emotions and yearning and spirituality of a kind previously hidden or non-existent.

By the time of Beethoven, it must not be forgotten, Europe enters an epoch of rich musical composition. It is also the period of Schubert and Schumann, and the deepening of the relationship between words and music in the flourishing art of Lieder. Goethe and the other great poets in their turn make demands on the music to express subtler and subtler ideas, something that was not happening in opera. With Beethoven a point is reached which involves not a development but a leap into a new dimension of communication. Beethoven appears before the world like a roaring lion. There is no compromise, no aesthetic to be negotiated, what is involved is the manifestation of the man, Beethoven, revolutionary, post-Christian, alone, the heroic embodiment of struggle and the refusal to accept suffering as the basis of man. Triumph over the intolerable odds of pain and mortality and social injustice and loneliness, this is the great diapason of victorious humanism that Beethoven was to pour into his opera, his sombre and powerful piano works, the nine questing sym-phonies and in his own transvaluation of all values the intimate testament of his quartets, his legacy to the future.

The much discussed last movement of the Ninth, when the symphony floods its banks and bursts into song, is taken as the point in which the symphony could no longer express the idea without words. This is a crude critical device which indicates an inability to examine the music and its quite original methods. The Eroica is just as coherent an intellectual and philosophical statement without words and the incomparable Fifth makes its inescapable confirmation of life in pure musical language.

The Missa Solemnis, which is commented upon musically in König's Ninth where he presents two units of a 'Mass' using Nietzsche's text, made perhaps the most radical demonstration that Beethoven had reached a point in his own and music's development where he could express himself ideologically, so that to listen to his Mass was to listen to the celebration of Overman doctrine, not to Christian anthropophagism. And this was exactly the message of the Nietzsche Mass of König's Ninth.

There is no escaping the message of Beethoven, and its simplicity does not diminish its power. The enormous emotional and spiritual impact, the clear simple nobility of the message is never separate from our awareness that it is Beethoven speaking. He is a universal man, titanic, almost mythic – it cannot be escaped, this bigness of the man, this thing, this non-thing that is called greatness. However much modern writers have played at psychiatric biography to diminish his human stature they have merely ended up enhancing it, making us love him more, admire him more – reach out with him, to what he reaches out.

The Wagner phenomenon, 'le cas Wagner', takes the Beethoven revolution one step further. Again we find ourselves with one political terminology and another musical one, but following for the moment the König thesis which is that the man and his art are not separable, let us unify the concepts and define the two men as revolutionaries. Or let us dispense with this term and settle for the word 'radical'. They are radical in their passionate conviction and upholding of the view that society needs to be transformed utterly, not reformed but renewed. It is this deeply felt conviction that man has been enslaved and needs liberating that lies at the heart of these two great composers. It must not be forgotten, as Frieda Ludendorff emphasized, that Mozart, Beethoven and Wagner are all monetarist victims. All three suffered most acutely from economic degradation and victimization. Each in his way defied the power system and identified with the new forces that turbulently swirled around them calling for new values. The link between Beethoven and Wagner is inevitably both musical and political, and when we say political we subsume economics under it. Wagner confirmed the link in his symbolic act of opening his theatre in Bayreuth, which was to be the home of the new music-drama, with a performance of Beethoven's Ninth, which he himself conducted. There is no doubt that he saw a step between the symphonic form as employed by Beethoven, which in turn reached its furthest limit with the Ninth, and his mythic epic, The Ring. Nor should it be forgotten how the whole German musical community collaborated and felt involved in the titanic creation of the Ring Cycle, how, for example both Brahms and Liszt modestly assisted in copying out orchestral parts to help in the mounting of the epic on time.

Richard Wagner had not only been an active political revolutionary and worked alongside Bakunin but had been branded as a terrorist and was a hunted man who had to flee across Europe to safety. People who are lofty about his hiding under the peacock's tail of the decadent Ludwig of Bavaria should not forget that his credentials as a radical are so powerful that to this day it is seen fit to censor his literary texts before the public can be allowed to read them. It is ironic that the society which makes such an issue of freedom of speech should need to remove from Wagner's texts those passages which make it afraid. The uncomfortable fact is that Wagner saw exactly what was happening about one hundred years before anyone else did. He wrote about it, and sarcastic rejection of his written work because of verbosity is hardly relevant. The truth is that Nietzsche was rejected also and he wrote some of the most beautiful German prose of all time. The content of Wagner's essays both in aesthetics and politics is very far-reaching. What Wagner described, firstly, was the direction in which the musical theatre should go. Secondly he outlined why it would not happen and who would stop it. Thirdly he basically confirmed the Nietzschean doctrines, despite contaminating them with Schopenhauerian pessimism in his later years.

Account had to be taken of the social factor influencing these men's lives – exhaustion. Wagner was exhausted not just by his tremendous labour as a creative artist creating the most gigantic artistic work known to man, the Ring Cycle, but also by his existential struggle to survive and display his creations to the world. Beethoven's struggle is of the same nature, and Nietzsche's was so harrowing that it cost him his mental equilibrium and eventually his sanity. These men were at war with society as then constituted, each one experienced a degree of fame, Wagner more than the others, yet they were all three abused and insulted and slandered by people who did not want these irresistible forces loosed on the minds of the new generation.

Wagner stated in clear terms that the musical theatre of the future needed to go down into the depths of the human psyche and into its prehistory until it met the bedrock of valid myths which would speak to the new post-Christian society about the fundamental crises and impulses of life in a way that would offer them that same 'katharsis' that the Greeks had known of old. At the same time that he called for this, and pointed the way, he also warned that the usurious forces in society could not allow this to take place for it would create a strong society that would reject monetarist domination. What he foretold was that these same forces working in society would create another kind of theatre and in place of his archetypal music-drama which would be a populist and folk phenomenon there would be a rootless entertainment, a 'musical' without drama in the ancient sense of confronting man's depths of being and mortality, which would replace that element with erotic dancing and in place of psychological confrontation and transformation there would be cheap novella-like love story and adventure. The trivialization of the music-drama into the musical comedy would mean the destruction of the culture and deliver the masses into the hands of the usurists.

His creation of the Ring was not unconnected to these reflections, they were the ideological base from which he worked. The Ring, being a myth, can be read at many levels and this is not incorrect but was exactly what Wagner wanted, to release the intellect to see beyond the surface phenomena to 'read' the events of history, in that same manner that Pound did with his epic poem dredging up his evidence from ancient China and early America. There is no way, however, in admitting it as a drama of the psyche or of ancient forces, that one can reject its clear political message. It openly declares that will to power is the driving force of politics. It openly reveals that the private psyche's intimate crisis can translate itself into the thrust of historical event. It openly dramatizes the theme that the price to be paid for controlling wealth and power is to fail to be loved. The cry of the usurers that they have suffered most cruelly does not make us love them, they cannot be loved. On the other hand it does not say that money or love of money is the root of all evil, Wagner was much too profound, for he shows how it is not necessary to own the gold at all. The gold throughout the vast drama, after it is stolen, lies hidden in a cave guarded by a dragon. It is enough to possess the Ring and the Tarnhelm, and when the Spear is possessed it must be broken. Siegfried in breaking the Spear becomes the protagonist who must be destroyed and his destruction, far from being the weakness of the saga some people imply, is one of its deepest insights. Siegfried is destroyed by deceit and deception, his heroic and dynamic energy is taken up by Brünnhilde because she sees that while deceit and deception are themselves the stuff of politics, there is possible another politique and she employs it – the result is the destruction of Valhalla and her enemies. In the truest sense they are a heroic couple, they are the new man and the new woman. Siegmund-Sieglinde are the ideal erotic couple, as Ludendorff pointed out, not implying that the couple of the future would be incestuous but that the quality of the man-woman relationship of the future would be collaborative like a brother-sister bonding, and therefore they provide the right foundations for the Overman. He is orphaned and this in turn provides the other necessary element of the Overman, that his higher self is drawn out of his own inwardness and is not projected on him under the spell of the eternal recurrence of the same, his father's super-conscious. Equally he has to discover the mother image as a friend and not a biological enemy, and so he is able to recognize the maternal in Brünnhilde and does not have to flee from it or punish it. The heroic pair echo the erotic quality of the twin-parents but it is not of the same intensity, in its place is an astonishing new element in the man-woman relationship fully made coherent for the first time. They are political partners, he leaves on his journey without guilt. Ironically critics complain of him going off and leaving Brünnhilde at home, this is the bourgeois conception of woman as wife-mother to the man. Wagner had no doubt that companionship was the most mature bonding possible between man and woman and it is little known that far from seeing women in a Tristan-Isolde trap he insisted that he had never known such an experience, and that the opera would suffice in place of a real life all-for-love experience. 'Tristan and Isolde' is for katharsis not imitation.

The balance between his work and his life is most satisfactory, for in the Ring Siegfried actually marries his aunt, and Brünnhilde is immensely mature in her responses to life. Also, significantly, Ludendorff points out that she has been 'put to sleep' so that between her and her father's image there is a hiatus, a psychic break which frees her for a full non-paternal love of Siegfried or whoever 'awakens' her so that he is her 'first' man. In life, as everyone knows, Wagner found enormous consolation and comradeship in the company of Cosima who was a much younger woman.

The seal of Wagner's balanced and compassionate world-view is his paean of praise to human love, to music and poetry, to German art (which weds the philosopher and the musician), and so overflowing is it in its generosity that it engulfs both friend and foe. Hans Sachs is a creation of such reflection and human affection and wisdom that he alone would have assured the work, but it contains also a deep love for the German people in their capacity to celebrate together not just human love but life itself in harmony and comradeship, at such a level and with such ecstatic beauty that it speaks not just for Germany but for the human species. This is the achievement of 'Die Meistersinger'.

Before coming to the importance of Wagner as the forerunner of a new music and a new theatre, Wagner as radical thinker, it is important to emphasize his significance in this development of music as a language and means of communication. As grammar gives the deep structure of language so harmony gives the deep structure of music. Wagner's chromaticism, however, is not his only distinction – the wide spread of sound in the Wagnerian chord is merely a characteristic. There are other elements which have to be identified that make up his musical framework. Transformation is one of the most complex and effective means in his musical methodology, a means he continued developing throughout his creative life. Allied to transformation is the motif, or leit-motif, a name given by others, although the identification of these musical tags or signifiers is disputable. They have almost the character of sub-atomic energy which can be measured as wave or as particle. The significance of the motif is not as an identifier, we do not need a flourish to announce the arrival of Wotan or Siegfried, but what the motif does because of how it is expressed is indicate to us the stage of that person's development, or the weight of that dramatic element, Ring or Spear, in the drama. Fate imposes itself and comes up from the darkest undertow of existence because of the foreground action. It is chthonic, ancient and asleep and does not want to emerge, for to emerge is to destroy, cut lifelines and annihilate. Wagner's towering genius, totally original, is to find a musical grammar for the interplay of personal action and political tension. From the early Rheingold to the final grandeur of Götterdämmerung this language complexifies so that in the former the transpositions from personal conflict (Wotan/Fricka) to political crisis in the confrontation with the Giants retain a certain simplicity, but through the whole cycle these relationships become more intricate and enlaced and inescapable, so that by the time audiences encounter Hagen they are prepared to enter directly into the most serious emotional and political engagement with his dilemma. It is not the fabric of the text which has enriched itself but the fabric of the music. Wagner needs the traditional constructions of the fourth part, and it is not true except in the crudest formal sense that he has 'written an opera' after all, since he had a purpose in this, for it cannot even be understood except by a complex and far-reaching set of already established back-references to the total set of motifs that have passed through the whole cycle. The result seems to be a kind of thickening of the Wagner sound, but what has happened is that his modifications of already familiar material, done to indicate deep character change and active forces at work, have altered our perception of his Ring-world. The music retains just the same chromatic principles as in the first part, the great opening chord to which Gorka paid homage in his First Symphony, is meant to take us to the great dying fall of the last notes which also opened his First. With this the doctrine of eternal recurrence of the same is confirmed, and pessimism, despite the perilous Schopenhauerian influence imposing itself more and more, is negated in favour of the extraordinary experience the public have at the end of the cycle – that life is going to begin all over again. The new liberated and leaderless class who by the devaluation of old values in the destruction of Valhalla and the old gods inherit the earth, must now create their own elite and by the will to power de-equalize their society, for equality is the fact of the lowest common denominator, just as will to power is the triumph of the highest common multiple. One might say that what happens between the end of Götterdämmerung and the beginning of Rhinegold II is what produces the new Wotans and Fafners, Frickas and Loges, the contract to build the new Valhalla. It is nothing less than the intellectual theme of the young König's First Symphony.

The price of this tremendous vision into the depths of Being and the nature of how things are was inevitably high. Wagner, exhausted, sank into the personal consolation of his Schopenhauerian sadness which is that last inaccessible haven of the Parsifal myth. Nietzsche, as always dazzlingly correct intellectually, with his intense emotional ferocity denounced Wagner as betraying that great vision he had formerly experienced and which produced his Overman music-dramas. Yet he himself was to seek refuge in madness as Wagner was to seek it in mysticism. The nineteenth century was a gigantic conflict which did not climax until the next. These two masterminds were ahead of their age, and looking forward into the future for the sake of mankind. What they saw and said would happen, happened. They were the enemies of barbarism, and the champions of human knowledge and wisdom. Nietzsche had written: 'What I desire is that the genuine concept of the philosopher should not utterly perish in Germany.' The dominant internationalist culture after 1945 had virtually silenced König's father and both ensured that he was not taken seriously and warned that he should not be. In the end Gorka König's struggle was that people would listen through the language of his music to those same ideas.

What König throughout his musical career wanted to say was that the tradition of German music and philosophy had not died, was central to civilization, yet had been halted and silenced. It had to be renewed, taking up again its themes of metaphysics, politics and ontology, most of all this last, for he also believed that his father had 'read' Nietzsche in such a way that the new generation could at last grasp that fiery torch and move again through the materialist darkness of usurist nuclear tyranny towards new values.

Gorka König had met Webern and been ignited spiritually by him. Despite the early vulgarities of the Second and Fourth Symphonies, which were in a sense his flirtation with Mahlerian over-sensibility and a youthful taste for Hollywood histrionics, König's musical inheritance and style itself derive from Webern. For this reason it is necessary to look briefly at his place in modern music.

Webern began his musical life as a pianist, interestingly, for that is how König came to him. He received his musical instruction from Edwin Komauer. He completed his studies of musicology and composition, at the Klagenfurt Humanistisches Gymnasium and later at the University of Vienna where he took his PhD. In those early years Wagner made a profound effect on his musical and therefore intellectual sensibility. He was a pupil of Schönberg from 1904, he received his degree in

1906. By 1908 the Schönbergian influence had come to an end, although there is no doubt that his youthful spirit responded to the Schönbergian attempt surgically to heal the gaping wound that Wagner had opened up in front of composers by creating a music that revealed the psyche and its strong tide of emotions.

The Stefan George song cycle (1908–09) saw the emergence of Webern's own musical identity. He married in 1911, there were four children. During these years he was engaged as a conductor. His own philosophy was certainly religious, but he was against the priesthood and loathed church dogma. In that sense he was a child of the Nietzschean revolution. He needed a complete renewal of his musical language, a revitalization, a transvaluation of all values. Webern found this in the important re-assessment that Schönberg made in the basic concepts of chromaticism and sequence-technique that was his Wagnerian and Brahmsian inheritance. His experiments and ultimately his creation of a new language in the twelve-tone system represented to Webern that necessary Nietzschean awakening. There is a direct correlation between Schönberg's passage from atonal to twelve-tone music and Webern's, the one following the other almost immediately into the new expression.

Webern enlisted in 1915 to serve his country but was discharged because of bad eyesight. This left him free to continue his activities as a composer and conductor. The attempt to impose Dollfuss up front while Hapsburg return fantasies were played out behind the scenes resulted in the League of Nations' agreement with Austria that it abstain from Anschluss with Germany until 1952. Another example of the mythic nature of so-called international law, invoked quite arbitrarily by its inventors only when required, according to König. It was during these turbulent years that Webern was invited to conduct in Switzerland, Germany, Spain and Britain. By 1933 Schönberg had left Austria for the United States. The German government declared the New Vienna School of which he was the founder to be cultural bolshevism and degenerate art. In 1938 came the annexation of Austria and with it poverty for Webern. As the Russian army approached Vienna he fled with his wife to Mittersill, near Salzburg. There, on 15 September 1945, he was shot dead in the doorway of his own house by an American soldier.

Webern's output is small but it makes a remarkable bridge from the re-defined twelve-tone structure of music to the earlier tradition of German music. Webern connects. While Schönberg starts again as it were, Webern also goes back to the beginning, that is to Bach, and this dynamic encounter with Bach and his spirituality as well as his music, gives enormous significance to this small oeuvre. When Webern ordered the young König to go back to Wagner and take up the challenge of his new language, König intelligently did not interpret this, despite his youth, to be an order to follow the musical style of Wagner, but rather re-engage with the Wagnerian weltanschauung, and with the dialogue that music could provide between the man and his time and between man and Time itself, or Being. Both Being and Time were the dominant themes of his father's philosophy, and the musical meditations of Webern were muscular, and olympic in their physical tonality, pared down, powerful, able to assault the heights of metaphysical speculation and statement. The new tonal freedom restored health and vigour to the Parsifalian exhaustion of late Wagner. But it did not break with the great Goethean dialogue between art and idea that had been the special genius of the Germanic people. It was most fitting and most fruitful that the young König should have been launched by the dry doctor of Vienna, Anton von Webern, for König in obeying his mentor's command to go back to Wagner did not become a Wagnerian, but rather a convinced Webernian.

In doing so he struck out for new territory and

he regained that Wagnerian initiative which took music as a means to explore the human psyche and therefore its politics, raising in the end those ultimate questions of a metaphysical nature which in the König reading of Nietzsche are in fact the primary basic questions from which stem one's politique and thus the kind of psyche one chooses to create.

One would be omitting another musical dimension in König's broad absorption of his Germanic tradition if one did not take into account also his debt to the Lieder tradition, especially in those groupings of songs like Schubert's 'Die Winterreise' and 'Die schöne Müllerin', and Hugo Wolf's 'Goethe-Lieder'. From them he learned that intricate phrasing which allowed him to imbue so much feeling in such apparently intractable material as the aphorisms and terms of his father's exalted ontology. The simplest melodic curve could lend depths and at the same time clarify a phrase with psychological insight if one took a leaf out of the German Lieder Book, something which König did with his usual openness and lack of fear that his musical acquisitions would ever seem to be pastiche, this was something he had also learned was possible from Ezra Pound both in his work and his aesthetic. Thus König's music is rich with references in the same way that 'The

Cantos' or Eliot's 'The Waste Land' are, and in such a manner that the material is assimilated into the new statement.

Thus with these many elements Gorka König created his ten symphonies. Against bitter opposition he stood his ground and insisted on the return to his society once more of the questing discourse of Being, and with his music he reached beyond words to celebrate the future and the growth of man.

Chapter Five

Frieda Ludendorff: An Interview

This is a transcript of Frieda Ludendorff's only interview on Bavarian radio.

INTERVIEWER: Dr Ludendorff, we would like to welcome you onto our programme. You come to us with a double reputation, if you will permit me to say so, first as the distinguished psychiatrist whose writings and whose clinical practice among autistic children is renowned, and second as the wife of the composer Gorka König. In both capacities you are, it seems to us, a most controversial figure. With your permission we would like to address some of these areas of controversy and debate tonight.

DR LUDENDORFF: Thank you. If we go into areas of controversy we will not clarify matters but obfuscate them. Areas of dissension are rarely enlightened by discussion. If you wish to know more of my position we should address ourselves to those areas of discourse that we may survey with equanimity.

INT: Er, quite. Dr Ludendorff, you are accused with your husband in many circles as being right wing? Are you?

LUD: Is the accusation made by the right wing? This language of right and left is a Jacobin dialectic, and I do not side with the right or the left but rather I oppose the forum itself, and its questionable legitimacy in Europe today. All this sustains the myth of democracy.

INT: Ah – you are opposed to democracy?

LUD: What democracy? Greek democracy, the collective decision of a small elite, and one which, we should not forget, was responsible for the death of Socrates, precisely because he was considered a threat to the democratic system? It also in our time has shown little compunction in condemning its greatest poet to incarceration in a lunatic asylum. Is there some model of democracy that you find acceptable? Certainly nobody would be taken in by English democracy, it is more class-controlled than ancient Greece. Which is the democracy you wish me to confirm?

INT: 'It may not be very good but it is the best that we have,' I think that is Churchill's observation.

LUD: Dubious logic from a dubious source. Faute de mieux is the argument of fools, in this case a most sinister one. I think you mean modern electoral democracy.

INT: Quite.

LUD: This I would define as the rule of the masses through a predictable mathematical method of control by that hidden elite which defines its parameters and its lines of communications. I have personally never met anybody who believed in politicians or their parties. Furthermore, it is known that the institutions themselves, congresses and parliaments, do not have substantive power over the monetary system or the military machine, these two zones are located outside their effective control.

INT: Was or is your husband a Nazi?

LUD: He was never a member of the National Socialist Party. He was a friend of Hitler over about two years. He has never denied this.

INT: Then he condones all the unspeakable horrors committed in Hitler's name during the Nazi regime?

LUD: Why must we use this inquisitorial language of hysteria? I am a psychiatrist. If it is unspeakable it is – usually – a fantasy. All human acts can be spoken of and confronted. People are clinically responsible for what they have done, not for what other people have done. Do you accept responsibility for all the genocide committed by the post-war system inside the USSR – which is 'your' ally, in Indo-China and Korea, Palestine, and so on? Do you accept that you created the atomic weapon to destroy the Third Reich and now have put the whole world in peril by your continued production of such weaponry? The crimes of the 'fifties and 'sixties are much more terrible for humanity than anything that ever happened in the 'thirties or 'forties. All human suffering is of the same quality, there can be no special case unless you wish to claim some mystical religious basis for it. I, as a scientist, cannot be a party to that view.

INT: Your husband has been deeply influenced by and uses the techniques of the New Vienna School, yet the Nazis banned their works and denounced their techniques.

LUD: Webern worked under the Nazis. He was executed by the Americans.

INT: Dr Ludendorff perhaps we can come to something less controversial –

LUD: That was my suggestion. . .

INT: In your writings you have spoken of a relationship between the crises of the psyche and the political conflict.

LUD: Well, of course there must be a relationship or we would be positing insanity as a norm which it is not yet entirely. The burning crisis issue of today is the irrationality of the monetary system and the interest basis of that economy, both in the usage of worthless promissory note money which cannot be transformed into real wealth, and through its banking and market structures. These have a built-in scenario of disaster since they are not connected to physical value, gold and silver, land and commodities. The figures are in the realm of fantasy. One could even go as far as to say that the monetary system was the direct product of a type of personality which required not the fantasy wealth, but much more dangerously, to be found out and punished. We are talking about guilt. Unfortunately, the guilty have designed a punishment system as extreme as their criminal fantasy. The 'being found out' scenario would involve an escape route through a nuclear war, a prospect which you and I do not relish, but many sick people prefer to the intolerable banality that comes at the end of fantasy. If people are not loved, and people who retire utterly into fantasy remove from themselves the dialogue of love, then they prefer destruction to abandonment. The usurious elite have placed themselves in this dilemma with us as their hostages. This is the real terrorism of our time, not that of rebels or police, both innocent victims along with the rest of the world.

INT: But are you saying this is a psychiatric problem?

LUD: Personal neurosis is always an ethical problem. This can always be solved. The political malaise on the other hand has a psychotic foundation. The argument of solving the world's problems today through institutions which cannot get at the causes and are actually designed to guarantee that the causes are hidden – is itself invalid. In a psychosis the first rule is not to listen to the 'plot', to the crisis scenario – 'I am being followed by Martians, the whole city is bugged, I am not really here I am on the moon'. One must ignore the urgent and hysterical message and observe the patient's own state in relation to those around him. If I cease to be panicked by anti-Nazi propaganda, pro-democratic rhetoric, right-left conflict, revolutionary movements, war in the stars, what do I find? I find that a robbery is going on, under my nose, a country's wealth is being taken by a group of internationalists without allegiance to any nation, more than that, the world's wealth – and it is in the hands of men who are not answerable to any elected government in the world and who were not appointed by any identifiable franchise in the world. I find that the exchange of worthless paper for world control is a powerful criminal act. I find that the inability to react is a serious psychosis which the masses today suffer. My experience with autism confirms for me that extreme psychotic phasing is a conditioned response to an uncondi-tioned illusion of freedom that is itself emotional slavery and absence of love. When the patient is given responsive signals which confirm his or her own reality then at that moment the cure is emergent, and no cure emerges in a psychiatric situation without the criminal being unmasked at the same time. We make ourselves neurotic – that is we twist ourselves – but we cannot enslave ourselves – that requires another or others.

INT: What is the solution?

LUD: What is the question? Here we come to the importance of Johann König's contribution not only to my personal life but to his age. We have to re-open the philosophical discourse that was punitively censored by the victors, I do not mean the allies, but those they were dying for, so that we can experience historical continuity. I am not saying re-read Nietzsche, but rather 'read' him in the new sense, using the guidelines that König set down in his Notebooks, for there is no doubt that he – with the focus of distance – sees things with a new vision. He has indicated that the metaphysical dialogue of European culture which began with Plato and Aristotle comes to its final end with Nietzsche's nihilism. This opens the door on ontology, and that implies irresistibly a new theological beginning rising out of the ashes of Judaeo-Christian decadence and giving the world a fresh and dynamic force of new life.

We must begin with the fundamental basic issue, and from that in a whole and integrated manner the politique must emerge, the new will to power must exert itself and it has a titanic task. Not only to destroy the old usuristic values but in destroying the old to save the earth itself from the psychotic revenge of the usurists. Ecologists cannot save the earth, they are themselves the tools of the usurists who set up ecology to ensure that it never became a threat to the usurious system. When the politique emerges then the justice system will emerge. Again, however, we must emphasize that our view is not utopian. Utopianism, too, is the instrument of the usurists.

We must act in our total freedom – totally conditioned, historically, biologically, environmentally, psychologically, physically, and yet in a ground of Being which is our unique and untouchable reality. We may do or we may not do – that is not our demand for freedom – we will do what we must do and we did do what we have done and we are doing what no one else can do and this is our uniqueness before Being and our immortality and our heaven and our hell and our agony and our bliss. I am already dead and buried for my past cannot even be dug up and I am unborn for my future is not even discernible, and now, although almost intolerable, is my one glorious reality, victory and only Truth.

INT: Could you say something of the Overman?

LUD: This is a key concept for today. Its archetype may have already existed in the past, but if so he must be identified as a historical figure and not a mythic one. Jesus is a mythic being who in the end takes his meaning from meta-historical claims made after his death, that is how Christianity proved to be a pseudo-religion as unmasked by Nietzsche. He also must be recreated for the future project which is man himself, not mankind as a species. My own conviction is that the Overman is not Overman unless a woman stands beside him, and, this is significant, after him, as companion and guardian of his truth. She is not less nor more – but the two make a pair – they do not have a biological duty but a role-model duty for the rest of the species.

There is a lot of basic material on this psychology to be explored in Wagner and his writings. You know, I suppose, that when he died he was engaged on a paper defining the new woman. This view we must say is as far from so-called feminism as the cult of woman as holy mother. He went beyond not only the ancient folk view of women but most emphatically he evolved a view of women quite unacceptable to the Victorian age. Like all great visionaries he had all the key elements right at the beginning but he had to free himself from the educational mis-information and his own psyche's indulgent longing for sleep on the maternal breast. From the Flying Dutchman to Götterdämmerung is a remarkable journey. His own transformation of the mythic material begins in Lohengrin. In eschewing the happy ending he makes, as well as a more satisfying drama, an awakening in the audience to the woman's point of view. We have to protest – she has been unfairly punished. This makes us question the lofty goal of Lohengrin. Yes, he has to fulfil his mission, but also she has to ask the question about his identity, she has a right. If he cannot trust her to stand by him he does not deserve her, not the reverse. It is not the woman who is tested in Lohengrin but the man. Wagner was simply not able to answer the problem at that stage. That he could ask it in the nineteenth century is awesome!

In the Ring Cycle his survey of women is perhaps unsurpassed in the complexity and depths of its psychological material. The Norns are women, worn down by the weight of their knowledge, pessimistically convinced that the great heroes and gods lack the will to power to free themselves from all their unprocessed psychic bondage. Wotan's wife Fricka is a very fascinating achievement, where Lohengrin gets away with his heroic role without having to be answerable to women, Wotan does not. Fricka confronts Wotan with his own actions in a way that only a woman who knows a man intimately, can do. The option in Christian society is at that point for the man to run away, and for the woman to indulge in Bovariste escapism. The confrontation between Wotan and Fricka remains musically and textually a lucid exposition of what the moral partnership is between a man and a woman. Being directed by men, and often rather odd ones, the opera has not in my experience been presented in the way the text and the music insist.

The Siegmund-Sieglinde model is even more disturbing to the bourgeois public. They like to be shocked at the incest and then show their broad-mindedness by declaring they forget it, so delightful is the love scene. The material is mythic and its resonance in us is that we recognize a perfect balance between man and woman which allows of immediate and climactic sexuality. These elements are against all the views of both the feminist and the anti-feminist. What are they? The quality of the encounter is based on the immediate element of recognition. Beneath this lies their being brother and sister. She takes him in, a stranger, and feeds him. He is in danger, she hides him. She shows him a sword embedded in a tree which is to prove the means of their liberation since it will render him invincible. She longs to be free of her tyrannical partner. Inspired by her he embarks on the psychic politics of freeing Sieglinde. He draws the sword. The sword is the instrument of taboo as it is in Tristan, which once removed gives them licence to be lovers. Wagner celebrates both the society which places taboos between men and women and the necessary act of being free of them. In this Nietzsche recognized Wagner's grasp of the

Dionysiac force. Yet the wisdom of Wagner is his understanding that the society is moving to barbarism which will smash all the taboos and offer an illusion of sexual freedom which will in fact enslave men and women to such a degree that the only restraint on their sexual behaviour will be micro-biological. Ironically, the Dionysiac Nietzsche wrote that he put on gloves when he read the score of Tristan, clearly afraid of the inescapable arousal of sensuality in the music. So we would identify that sameness is an erotic quality, the oppositeness is biological, the appearance and the psyche are the same. This is the opposite of the decadent modern view, which is why some people end up seeking a partner who is the same biologically just in order to find a partner who has sameness of psyche and appearance, which of course is not a solution.

Wotan is another masterly achievement of psychological analysis. Apart from the exact and moving delineation of Wotan as father, as husband, and as man alone, he remains the most deeply explored creation in modern art of man as homo politicus. This is a completely Nietzschean projection and one must not forget that despite the famous polemic Nietzsche himself is the first Wagnerian, and his rejection of Parsifal does not diminish this. In Wotan we see man rising to power and then instead of fulfilling himself through himself and his own will to power he makes the fatal mistake of trying to buttress and confirm his power by outward means. To be powerful he needs an arena in which to disport himself. Valhalla. To build Valhalla he needs to enlist the Giants, that is, enter into a dangerous alliance. To satisfy them he needs wealth. To pay his unpayable debt he undermines the very basis of his class power, for the ransom for non-payment is the Goddess who supplies the Gods with their life-sustaining food. His solution is the theft of the Rhinegold. In all that follows what is significant, from a Nietzschean point of view, is that Wotan loses will to power when he enters the pragmatic move-by-move chess-board of political machination in which every move is for the future and defers crisis to the future, but increases with each move the gravity of the crisis and diminishes the possibility of there being any future. In all this of course we see the folly of Western nuclear policy with its perilously naive doctrine of deterrence. As he becomes enmeshed in the necessary he loses the capacity for spontaneous and free action which alone can liberate the world.

We are living through an epoch of just such politics, we are in an age of arena politics, vast arenas and small men. Great international conferences in mighty venues where the protocol and display of power hides the utter helplessness of the participants to alter the situation. The picture is for public consumption, for the men of power are out of the 'picture'. How moved we are by the entrance into Valhalla, for we know it is a disastrously wrong action. What is important is that we should not sanction it in the halls of world political discourse. The issue is the gold, the slave-class which we now call the third world, and the corruption of the political system which is now without power, but that is another subject. If you will permit me I would like to return to my survey of the psychiatric importance of the Ring characters.

To me the Ring's central character is undoubtedly Brünnhilde. Again we need to see it produced correctly, and for this Siegfried should be of tremendous charismatic dynamism. Wagner makes such impossible demands on his singers, but for the Cycle to work Siegfried must be a thrilling and powerful figure. Brünnhilde completely clarifies the father-daughter relationship and the myth serves Wagner in this. The Wotan-Brünnhilde duologues contain enough for a whole book on the psychology of the father-daughter syndrome, both its incest and its creativity. It is the most rounded, and completed female creation in the art of the theatre, and much more interesting than anything in the novel. Brünnhilde with the Walkyries is for a woman very exciting, it is everything that is now repressed in the liberal ecologistic woman who competes with men. It is a celebration of the power of women and the wildness of women that is always exhilarating to women and a little scary to most men, although, fortunately, erotic to some.

When Wotan puts Brünnhilde to sleep on the mountain it marks their mutual renunciation of the biological incestuous bond. It involves a forgetting, and a renewal of the psyche in the man who awakens her. The awakening is most complex and has an ambivalent effect on the audience. They are not used to this kind of woman – here the actress must understand women to play it truly. For the third time in the Cycle we are asked to examine the human couple. Wotan-Fricka represent the bourgeois marriage. Siegmund-Sieglinde represent the erotic ideal, and therefore the new parental model. The third couple are frankly a most revolutionary pair. Critics make fun of the fact that they are actually nephew and aunt, but as a psychiatrist I rather like this! The elements to be confronted however are these: his being an orphan is an essential part of his being the Overman. It implies that if we are looking for a model of an Overman, in the past or future, we must expect him to be an orphan.

INT: Why?

LUD: Because he has formed his psyche without a biological imprinting of authority by the father and in the end has built up his own selfhood as best he could, thus it makes his psyche his own and utterly original, that means his spontaneity is not blunted. Equally, he has a memory of great love, the mother, but is not attached to it so that he cannot escape to it by going back to it or by projecting it onto a woman, then punishing in the wife the mother who betrayed him to the father, and also because in the deepest psychic sense she is not and cannot be the mother. Thus on encountering a woman he sees her utterly fresh like a new being. The famous 'This is no man!' of Siegfried when he first sees her is a great moment in western drama. Then his response that it is his mother is from a psychological view the adult response that must be made in order that it be surpassed. He consciously recognizes that it is not his mother. The bourgeois man meets his partner just as if it were another man for he only knows woman as mother. Then he is horrified that she behaves differently from a man so he treats her like his mother because inevitably that response will always work. In the Brünnhilde-Siegfried encounter exactly the opposite takes place. They are immediately open towards each other, again the details in the text merit full study, and approach sexuality with a vigour that is far removed from the mental dreaminess and fantasy atmosphere of Tristan. Brünnhilde confirms his project. They are bonded, a couple, and free.

The end of the saga is enormously rewarding within this framework I am proposing, which is Nietzschean, and the key to it is that the Gibechungs are the rising power elite and can only conceive of the man-woman relationship in terms of contracts and traps. This is part of the Wagnerian equation that will to power means the surrender of the capacity to be loved, unless one can produce a new and higher model of human life in which the highest will to power is motivated by man-woman love, not I must insist religious 'love' as in the Christian fantasy. In Brünnhilde's decoding the nature of political activity as 'drugging' its protagonists, and in determining to destroy the power elite because of their crimes, not just killing Siegfried but disturbing the natural basis of life, she takes on power.

Brünnhilde is the first person who takes the Ring into her possession and wills consciously not to possess it. Wagner's insight into the woman's psyche, and that this is her role, is a historic moment for the human race. That he found it embedded in an ancient myth is all the more inspiring. It is by her act that the cyclical life pattern is allowed to revolve again and the natural life flow can continue. In the nature of the will to power, maximum power must be sought again and the story re-enacted. Remember, neither Wagner nor Nietzsche is a utopian. There is no naive dream of a happy-ending life on earth with everybody walking around in a stupor of goodness and exaltation.

INT: The observation you have made of the qualities required for the new man and woman imply very radical re-appraisals of our views.

LUD: Absolutely. Leaving aside the disaster of the universities and their historical achievement in halting utterly the philosophical discourse, children's education at home and in the school is a recipe for human tragedy.

INT: Is this a hopeless situation, you make it sound like one? What are we to do?

LUD: We have everything we need in our own tradition. We could re-read again some of our own great thinkers with a view to benefitting from them, not just sitting and setting examinations on them. I find 'Wilhelm Meister' a radical text. There has always been in the past a special educational system to create an elite. Mass-education has left society without an elite. The old schools that once produced the elite of empire are of no use for the needs of today. The creation of a new elite is not merely a pedagogic problem, it will have to take into account those elements I have referred to in the metaphoric context of the Ring, for no school can produce an educated young adult unless the infantile and formative pattern of the self has been consciously modelled to break the biological imprinting that produces robotic repetition of the parental crime. We have many models of elite training and they each in their way confirm this principle. It is a subject to which I would like to apply myself. Having made a detailed analysis of the autistic response and found it almost a kind of norm that society has decided to tolerate, both at the societal and familial level, it clarifies for me what the alternative would be, the opposite. Except in the most superficial context spontaneity is dreaded in this culture. It is most interesting that the ruling element in society has no idea of giving its inheritors an education that would allow them to become more strong, and this is a clear sign that their will to power is exhausted. I would go as far as to say, that from a psychiatric point of view the condition of the usurious masters of the world is so fragile that – once the system is decoded – taking power is far from difficult.

INT: You are saying that it is easy to take power?

LUD: It has never been easier — of course, the masses think it has never been more difficult because they believe the scenario of the control mechanism. As long as you think money is real, you will be an obedient slave. Once you grasp that it is worthless you recognize poverty in the fantasy money system, and at the same time real wealth in the world's natural resources, the greatest of which is man and woman. 'The Emperor's Clothes' by Hans Andersen is another radical text.

INT: I would like to ask you about Gorka König. I see that the Königs, yourself included, seem to have the same view of life and society. Am I correct?

LUD: In the essentials, yes, but that is because we have thrashed the matter out among us, we have argued, made models and rejected them. We have arrived at certain conclusions. What depresses us somewhat is that you may discuss anything in the world but there are certain taboos on certain subjects which ensure — not only that these subjects are not broached — but if the propositions are made which are necessary to engage the issue then you are immediately defined as being not just inhuman, but the victim of a psychosis by which you translate your perverted aggressions into a political language which no sane person can tolerate. This is bad science and bad politics. There is a body of prejudicial definitions separating serious debate on the current crisis, there are a set of accusative terms which define you as intellectually unacceptable, psychologically impaired, and humanly barbaric if you attempt to step into the arena of critical discourse on which politics is dependent for genuine transformation. Until we brazenly challenge these arbitrary, unscientific and punitive rules, the defence system of the usurious elite, we cannot hope to change society. This is an issue which we – each one in a different discipline – have been aware of, so do not fondly imagine the situation exists as told on television discussion programmes, that there is freedom of speech and openness of discourse. Some writers are never published, some songs are never sung. Some poets are declared insane.

INT: Some philosophers. . . ? But Dr Johann König is free to lecture, publish his books.

LUD: Yes, to lecture, but people are so warned off in advance that they have to re-learn how to listen. Look at the American edition of his Nietzsche Notebooks. Quite without his knowing an insolent and derogatory set of essays was appended by his publisher to each volume. They were the work of someone who clearly did not grasp what the major thesis of the work was, and who had made the major issue of the validity of his subject's writing the degree to which König had dissociated himself from the Nazis, or was still a Nazi and so on and so on. The setting together of his arbitrary and highly personal value judgments and historical misreadings of history alongside his lamentable failure to understand the message of Nietzsche, let alone the interpretation of König, resulted in the final statement of the book being an assurance to the reader that he could discard the work and that it only had a marginal interest to a few academics.

INT: Has your husband's music suffered in this way?

LUD: No. The response to his music is universal. Here his opponents are put in a more difficult position but it does not stop them from adopting it. That is, he is a great composer, what a pity he has let himself get involved in matters that do not concern him, like politics, and for which he has no talent or temperament, and this eccentricity stemming from the same type of psychic weakness which marred poor Richard Wagner has prevented him from being the great master we would have been happy to have in our concert halls and on our television sets. As long as people think of him as a bit odd, and not intellectually sound, then we can talk of pure music and forgive him.

INT: The Tenth is such an intellectually taxing work yet it leaves one with a great serenity, with an emotion of depths and calm. This seems to have a religious quality about it. Could you comment on this?

LUD: Remember, the text is about man's being, a man's innermost essence, and how that essence has some particular relationship with Being itself. This, if you like, and here neither Johann nor my husband would let me say such simplistic things, is nothing other than that ancient religion which is the religion of the philosophers. On this subject it would be more fitting to examine Johann König's last paper on Ibn Rushd which has very radical implications. As a psychiatrist I would prefer to make another observation. That is, that just as neurosis is not a medical problem but an ethical one, and psychosis is a crime committed by others and therefore a political problem – I should add I am not talking about deficiency in brain capacity or lesion in brain tissue – so the psyche that is accepted as being a norm in society in its turn is lacking. There is an existential need which must be confronted. I do not consider this the material of the neurotic personality in the framework which claims 'we are all neurotic', that is a control concept. Let us define the neurotic as the person engaged in healing psychic wounds and historical traumata or avoiding them, these people have their own problem which can be isolated, identified and healed or made tolerable: they are the ones I would define as having an ethical problem for in the end their growth is dependent on ethical choices and programmes, not on insight as such. Much more serious and much more critical for the future of the species is the provision of a natural and simple framework which helps that ordinary, I do not like the term normal, and full personality identify and confront their mortality, their secret quality of uniqueness, their isolation, their having a destiny, and gives them a method by which they have daily, yearly and once in a lifetime actions which remind them, remind them, remind them of their identities in some ultimate way and connect them to Being itself. Without this the neurosis must be aggravated and enter crisis, and the society must open itself to fantasy projects which is what has happened to European culture since 1945, for whatever mechanisms it had before then have been devalued and destroyed. I am glad this has happened, and have no nostalgia for the past. I am however insistent that the future needs that simple frame which makes life possible and the present bearable. In order that this may happen one must depart from the correct philosophical launching pad, otherwise once in orbit the journey will be on the wrong trajectory. Again I repeat we have no destination but our journeying.

INT: If I have understood these observations, Dr Ludendorff, it surely means that composing music and pursuing psychiatry have in some way been gone beyond, there is some kind of dépassement, is that fair?

LUD: Quite right. So what now? Is that your question?

INT: Exactly!

LUD: One must live in constant renewal and in growth. I read that if the last day of the world came upon one when one was planting a tree one should continue to plant it. I think this is Overman philosophy. I think this power will prevail. My husband and I have a job to do. We are not different, he and I. He is a psychiatrist, his father was like a musician and I find my work is most philosophical, or 'we can all move down one please', in the end it does not matter. The usurists are not afraid of terrorists, they designed that model themselves to identify in advance opposition and isolate it. They are afraid of only one thing. They are not loved. Nobody loves them, even their defenders, even their collaborators. They have stolen the Ring, and so they have forsworn love. Gorka König and I have discovered the kind of men and women needed to liberate the world from this curse of usury. Let us create one spontaneous man and one aware loving woman and we can destroy them and bring down their plastic palaces in flames. We can kill the dragon and get the gold out from its cave where it lies useless and buried. We can decide that we do not want the Ring. This is ultimate will to power. So we are going to win. This is the work of the rest of our lives.

INT: Dr Ludendorff, thank you.

Chapter Six

König's Tenth

Now that some years have passed since the creation of König's Tenth Symphony the critical response at the time which hailed the work both as the pinnacle of König's symphonic creations and as a new beginning in musical expression has been confirmed not only by the public but by a growing literature of analysis and appreciation which, far from having diminished the status of the work, has set it as one of the great masterpieces and spiritual testaments of our time.

As well as its intrinsic worth it has also shown itself to have value as a guidepost to other composers and its influence is already being heard. König took music out of the cul-de-sac into which it had manoeuvred itself after 1945. As if in shock from the trauma of the war and the splitting in two of the European cultural heartland of Germany, music had broken into two paths as if in echo of the political condition of the land. On the one hand there had been an understandable retreat into a neo-classicism as if to pretend that nothing had happened and a modern polish to the old chromaticism was all that was required, and on the other the pursuit of Webern's serialism had systematized itself into a kind of monotony and structural rigidity.

While Webern had undoubtedly taken the musical syntax of Schönberg, he had gone beyond him in his own search for a continuity of the Wagnerian style, with a deep awareness of the long Germanic musical tradition including its isorhythmic techniques in early church music. His complex polyphony was strengthened by his capacity and taste for dividing parts of melodic phrases over several instruments lending texture, grace, and often depths to the musical statement. König had from his Fifth realized that Webern's stripping back music to its essential elements was the necessary point of departure for a new music. He in a sense also foresaw the trap of mathematizing the music beyond its capacity to express profound emotions and concepts. He had stayed inside the symphonic tradition in his first four works and won time for himself to contemplate the implications of a post-Brahmsian sound and its irrelevance to the modern condition, and the trap of a modernism that fell victim to a fascination for technology which could only end in the surrender of musical expression to the superficial art of revealing sonic machines' capacities to emit signals. Concrete, electronic and computerized music were precisely that, but the future of music depended on the use of its own established syntax, or its development. König made just such a breakthrough. By the time he had reached his Tenth he had not only firmly established himself in the post-serial techniques but had been driven to find a new expression for the deepening philosophical and emotional material which his own life and epoch had generated in him. With his last Symphony he was ready to make his clear statement, his testament, in a voice that was uniquely his own.

He consciously saw his place in music as one which wed in people's imagination two languages, two traditions, the two passions of his culture, music and philosophy. With his Tenth he produced their offspring, a coherent if complex philosophical statement in musical-grammatical language. As he had said: 'I want the voices to be instruments and I want the instruments to speak.' In this conceit he was able to encapsulate the deep artistic truth of his creativity. He had always insisted that the language of music had evolved to a remarkable degree. His father had pointed out to him that Kant had considered music as the lowest of the arts precisely because it was wordless, and had proposed that if it were wedded to poetry it could serve society. König's perception in this matter was deeper, being himself a musician before he became a philosopher, for he grasped that the music had 'found its voice', had become language. In his years in the wilderness of America he had studied musical form back to its Germanic medieval beginnings. He realized that the enormous respect for Bach the composer and genius had hidden from people Bach the setter of words, the lieder-master, curving the melodic phrase to the meaning of the text. Where others had explored the great architectural units of sound in the fugues and concertos, or simply stood back in awe of the emotional impact of the Passions and Masses, König scrutinized the narrative flow between Bach's choral passages, the use of the solo voice, and his strictly disciplined musical vocabulary in conveying information.

By the nineteenth century König, again in collaboration with his father, had found that the view of the philosophers had changed. Schopenhauer had gone as far as to say that music was not the copy of ideas but the copy of the will itself. 'That is why the effect of music is so much more powerful and penetrating than that of the other arts, for they speak only of shadows, but music speaks of the thing itself.' Schopenhauer's dictum convinced König that he was on the right lines. His discovery of the valedictory cry of Nietzsche licensed him to speak, 'New ears for new music!' He had written this over the title page of the Tenth on the day it was completed.

His musicological research had led him back to Bach, and his philosophical exploration under his father's tutelage had led him back through their own linguistic tradition out to the ancient Greeks. Yet in following that backward trek over territory which in its day had been virgin and dangerous and was now barren and deserted, he realized the Nietzschean claim that Christianity was anti-philosophical and in some way broke the intellect's capacity, for it removed its need. If people were arbitrarily saved from one point in time, and that saving was dependent on them knowing and believing that someone else had done their suffering and dying for them, then they no longer needed any philosophical discourse and therefore were cut off from that creative angst which drove a man to understand the depths of his own being. If the Greeks were to be 'read' by Christian thinkers – Thomist or Protestant, for Kierkegaard's 'leap' was across a byss not an abyss – it was an illusion, it was simply avoiding the great fact of Christianity's mythic anti-intellectual nature, embedded as it was in ancient animism as the nineteenth century had discovered, and that way no illumination of the metaphysical issue could take place.

König could understand how much it meant to Nietzsche to see Wagner heroically and alone go back before Christianity to the great Germanic myths and at the same time wed that to the epic drama of Aeschylus to give it structural and cathartic power. He could also see that the Lutheran attempt to renew Christianity by cleansing it of its theatre of blood sacrifice had forced Luther's theology back into a more conceptual zone, where thought again became at least possible. With the magical arena of buying and selling salvation through anthropophagic rites swept aside and with the rejection of the magical papal authority, Luther returned to a theo-centric doctrine which replaced Catholic drama with Unitarian emphasis on God and his will. The God of destiny and the Lord of Willing replaces at least in part the utter theatricality of Catholicism which the Thomists could not save, precisely because they had killed the Aristotelian method by trying to compromise it with impossible doctrines that could not be justified philosophically. Nevertheless König observed a wedding of that Lutheran theocratic view with the musical contribution of Bach. Bach made Jesus human, the music was divine. Bach also celebrated the volk, the congregation, as Wagner was to do later in all his operas, and most sublimely in Die Meistersinger von Nürnberg.

The philosophical tradition from Kant was one grounded in a deep spiritual conviction and a detached relationship with Christianity and its odd beliefs. The social inhibition was caused by a mythic religion which extolled a man supposed to be God who was in fact utterly helpless, in the most abject symbol of defeat, crucifixion. The transcendental 'good news' was of course bad news for men, and worse news for women. If man's role was to be helpless on a cross, woman's role was to be weeping mother. Luther's heroic revolt raised but did not solve these issues, nor, more tragically, did he release the people from the rule of a priest class. All that changed was that where before the monastery gave the authority to be a priest, now the university gave it.

Nietzsche's revolutionary role was to reject the total Christian ethos, the debilitating exaltation of pity as a human emotion, the sexual perversity of crucifixion mythology, the morality imposed from outside on the people, and the idea of a priesthood as retainers of truth. With 'Zarathustra' Nietzsche did not 'go back' to Lutheran dogma as Christian apologists liked to claim, he had pointed out that one of their techniques was to 'Christianize' any doctrine which they could, since they had no real philosophical foundation of their own. On the contrary, what he had done had been to demolish forever the illusion that Christian myth and its institutions held a future for mankind. Nietzsche opened the way to take up again a pure discourse on the ultimate nature of existence, of the self, and of Being, as the necessary steps to creating the Overman.

König saw his father's significance as being that he had recognized that with Nietzsche the Judaeo-Christian era was over, and that implied communism-capitalism. He had learned from Pound that the lynch-pin of that culture had been usury itself, and that only with the collapse or destruction of the monetary system could the world be freed not only from the intolerable debt system whose root it was, but also from the threat of nuclear annihilation, for this was the weapon of the internationalists. The whole world's population basically was against nuclear war and yet it was in the hands of an elite who would not hesitate to use it. Its victims were powerless to stop them since they were set up in nation states while the usury-elite were internationalists operating freely across the board of history. It was against this urgent and anguished background that König composed his Tenth Symphony.

What, embedded in that complex musical structure and in that difficult text, is the message of Gorka König's final testament to his age? In a way it is nothing less than his outline of what he considers to be the fundamental element in the education of a conscious man, or if you like the orientation of historical man towards his destiny to confirm the Overman. Therefore it represents the metaphysical foundations in the thinking of a new elite. In the machine age, with this awareness awakened and activated in them, and with these internal conflicts worked out, such men will be able to dominate and benefit from the technological transformation of nature without being destroyed by it, and find their own depths and identity in the ultimate confrontation with their mortality and their particular secret access to Being itself.

It offers that deep Goethean sanity which Nietzsche loved and ransomed in order to go beyond the contradictions of his age and clear the way for the new man. It calls to the youth of the new society to take on his fathomless profundity not by withdrawing in Buddhistic pessimism but by a structured inner journey which looks fearlessly into the dark vortex of the self and its fragile in-time helplessness against the cosmic spaces, and there dash himself against the rocks not of his fears but of the utterly indifferent total force and will to power of Being itself which makes no contracts and accepts no partners. Once annihilated to himself, and annihilated to that annihilation, he begins another journey, this time from non-existence back to existence, now robed with a robe of honour, confirming not himself although he has been into the utmost inner chamber of his own secret, but confirming Being itself from whose plenitude the myriad objects flow, without being like Being, or produced by Being, or diminishing Being. Unique in its endless wealth of creativity and isolated from any identification with its creations – Being declares itself on his tongue. But now he is a man who has looked on the real, and he has found that the secret of the smallest atom is the secret of the whole, and that the smallest particle itself contains the whole in its vastness, and its secret is not different from his secret, for he contains in himself the many worlds, the galaxies, and the far-flung starry sky beyond the limits of knowing and measuring. The whole universe is contained in him and swallowed up in him as he in turn is its speck of dust, its cosmic point, utterly obliterated and overwhelmed and hidden and vanishing between existence and non-existence, having come from non-existence and returning to it in the blink of an eye, free at last and able to confirm that he does not exist, is not, as it does not and is not, in the most uncompromising nihilism which has removed from itself its own ground of non-being, until this knowledge itself transforms its owner, as the lamp becomes lit from the oil within it and visible until it shines across all space by the glass that contains it, and when he illuminates with his illumination and is himself self-consuming light from a light that is never consumed and is not from here or there but is itself Light, then he is filled with knowing joy, flooding blinding dazzling knowing joy and bliss that pours out and is that same bliss that is nothing other than the movements and vibrations of the particles in their transformative force, always and forever existent and non-existent, not now here now not, but at the same time, hereness and thusness, and veiled by light upon light, Being itself, in its effulgent blinding sight-giving self-illumination. And the man of knowledge, the utterly humbled and shattered man of this station realizes that it is his universe, his stars, his moons, his prophets, his million armies marching across endless battlefields renewing and replenishing the earth with the force of will to power, from beginning to end it is all his and he does not exist, and it does not and there is nothing to say that can be said, and nowhere to go that can declare any other truth. And he is turned around, totally turned round. His heart is full of this great joy. Then he hides his secret and cloaks it and withdraws with it into silence. If he speaks it he will only suffer and the world will hate him as it loved him and reject him as it went to him until he learns by great trial and pain that it cannot be spoken and it belongs to its people, as the peacock only spreads its tail to its own kind. As he in his crisis swam in the cosmic ocean, lost, now he in peace swims in the ocean of his own heart.

This is the journey he calls on the noble youth to take. And then set out to war! unbeatable, unquenchable, with victory certain, and a vast serenity.

Chapter Seven

König's Decision

The disappearance of the Königs, Gorka and Frieda, one week after the first public performance of his Tenth Symphony in Berlin remains unexplained. They flew from Berlin to Hamburg, booked into the Atlantic Hotel, paying in cash on arrival. It seems that they did not spend the night there. They were last seen standing on the edge of a windy pavement outside the hotel that afternoon, waiting. A large BMW drew up, the couple got in and it drove away swiftly. They were never seen again.

It was inevitable that speculation would flare, with both serious and interested theories from their friends and admirers, into fanciful and politically melodramatic theories which seem to tell more about their authors than the subjects of their interest. Naturally, the first enquiries devolved upon their son and daughter. Eva who lived with her grandmother, now a legendary recluse, in southern California, had basically cut off relations with her parents and could shed no light on the subject, nor did she seem desirous of pursuing the matter. She expressed neither hostility nor anxiety. If that is what they wanted to do, then let them. Of one thing she was certain, they were not partners in a dual suicide, that was against everything she knew of her parents both temperamentally and intellectually. Even in the face of some unknown medical tragedy she knew with sure conviction that they would never consider self-inflicted death as a viable human option.

Their son, Anton, was equally unforthcoming, as if the persistent and insistent questioning of the media was before anything an invasion of his privacy. In the end to avoid the press who annually brought up the issue with the inevitability that they returned to the themes of Venice sinking and Pisa's tower leaning, Anton König issued a statement declaring that his parents had confided nothing of such a decision to him, and that if they had chosen anonymity after the long years of a fame which never gave them peace it did not surprise him. He echoed, as did all his friends, his sister's certainty that they were not candidates for a Meyerling suicide pact. People close to Anton König, now a young military officer, are convinced that he does know what has become of his illustrious parents, but equally sure that he will never tell.

The extreme political version is that they were murdered by a ring of international bankers who felt their influence was becoming too powerful and that at last the König view of interest itself, and not just the naïve idea of excess interest, as the cause of world crisis was being recognized as true. Certain powerful behind-the-scenes figures in American finance are mentioned. Others see the hand of communist ideologues who finally felt that with the Tenth, of all pieces, König had made himself a figure for the unification of Germany. With all these theories it depends on your point of view whether it was the CIA or the KGB or the internationalists who had eliminated their most influential and respected enemies, these two ageing and somewhat inaccessible intellectuals, who despite a mass public reputation remained remote from mainstream thought, still addressing themselves to an elite. On the contrary, argued these people passionately, yesterday they had been eccentrics, but the wheel of history had turned and now the time had come for their voices to be heard. It was a very necessary and meaningful act for their enemies to eliminate them, politically astute, and socially just in time.

There was also what the press called 'the white horse of Zapata theory'. This was, that they were not dead, but that they lived in hiding, awaiting the political uprising against the internationalist monetary elite and plotting towards that day. According to this legend the Königs had withdrawn to some desert placing their forces, person by person, in a world-wide network that when the moment came would strike, and in one night the computerized archive of the monetarists would be destroyed and the world's starving, poor and potential victims of nuclear war would break at last their fetters and be free to create a world based on real wealth, power, and justice for the intellectual elite as well as the oppressed. This became for them as strong a myth as the white horse that the peasants could still spot on the mountain-top assuring them Zapata was not dead and that freedom would one day return to Mexico. Such, and such, were the responses to this undoubtedly mysterious event. Music lovers simply regretted that this great composer was silent. The psychiatric profession missed hugely the ongoing debate with Frieda Ludendorff who had contributed such a lively and vitalizing quality to their discourse. One detail did not fail to elude them. Slowly and painstakingly over the months before the disappearance, Dr Ludendorff had wound up the analysis of those patients she was treating, or had arranged for their transfer to another doctor who followed her system.

Thus we can confirm the first certainty. The Königs did not commit suicide, unless there is some strange element of which we know nothing in their lives and thinking. The second certainty is that it was a premeditated decision, otherwise the clearing of the decks, attending to patients, packing a whole library of books and music, and the winding up of their recorded financial identities, do not make sense. The Freiburg house was settled on Anton König, and there are other details which friends and relatives seem to have closed ranks on, so that we cannot trace the clues. One third certainty exists – in the form of a letter which Gorka König wrote to a friend of his in Heidelberg, a professor of political psychology. Here is the relevant extract, never before made public. Let us give Gorka König, therefore, the last word.

> '. . . to sum up I am convinced that a process which began with the First World War (some would go back to the Boer War because the whole history of gold storage and diamond marketing begins there) found itself incomplete in 1919. The end of the war is a most strange matter and I am not satisfied with the official version, all the more so since it has in my lifetime been substantially rewritten. It is as if there had been a scenario, and with the fecund energy of historical forces that scenario had

been inhibited and uncompleted. So began that same process with a new strategy. Despite the ideologies involved it is a naked fact that America-Russia were and have proved to be the enemies of Germany. The one punishing us most brutally after the first great conflict and then acquiescing in allowing the other to cleave us in two after the second.

'Yet the vocabulary and syntax of power politics covers up the forward movement of events in this century. I no longer believe that an "America" exists, or a "Russia". Communist states are enmeshed in this monetary magic alongside the capitalist ones. We are locked into a dialectic from which we must escape — and this is your duty. There is a world to be saved. International institutions are powerless because the nation as currently defined and set up is powerless. We must pull back the curtain behind the puppets of politics and reveal the manipulators of power in the world today, those who control the world's mythic paper wealth, and through it own a vast hoard of real wealth in gold and diamonds. If we cannot reach this goal by rational argument and intellectual demonstration because the lines of communication have been so successfully severed by the new soft censorship, then nothing less than the redrawing of the world's map has to take place.

'I repeat that we are going to have to redraw the map of the whole world. We must break up the mythic and yet nuclear confrontation of Russia and America, and remove by this the hidden elite who thrive on this confrontation and fear. To this end we must redefine in a more natural way what a nation is. The abolition of constitutions, that recipe for surrender to monetarism, will pave the way for a more scientific view of nationhood, and it should be one which brooks no exceptions. At first analysis it is clear that the key elements are already known, while denied. A common geography, culture, language, and people make up a nation. The Basques are a nation, two constitutions, France's and Spain's, refuse them the much-vaunted rights they claim for themselves. The Sikhs are a nation. The Tibetans are a nation. The Turkoman masses imprisoned in southern Russia are a nation. The Pathan are a nation. The Tawareg are a nation. The Kurds are a nation. The American blacks are a nation. The Afrikaaners are a nation. The Palestinians are a nation. The Irish are a nation. There is a Germanic nation too, and it cannot be denied to make our enemies happy.

'Just think for a minute, in the vacuum of modern politics what a new wind blows for humanity in restoring true identity to peoples with frontiers drawn not by a hidden hand after an unconditional surrender but by men who decide what is best for the planet that life can flourish with real money and real trade and real cultural exchange. We must be finished with this awful sameness of a pseudo-culture designed by a people who are at the moment everywhere and yet nowhere at home, the internationalists, who have made Peking like Miami to hide their alienation in a world where they will never settle down for it is not their desire, their desire is only to possess power by magic, the magic of worthless usurious wealth. Oh my good friend!

'Do you not see? Do you not hear? Do you not feel the world groaning and crying out to be done with this heartless and valueless society that recognizes only deceit and ruthlessness in business transactions, sharks who have long since devoured the little creatures of the seas and now attack each other, do you not feel what is happening? I do, my friend. And something must be done. A voice must speak for simple life. For language. For customs. For sports and games. For local music. For the building of this place and the building of that. For the people.

Technology is neither a problem nor an enemy. It is this madness that is called usury, with its weapons of death and its doctors of death that must be faced by the new generation.

'I know of no worthier cause. Yet I do not see it emerging unless it is also grounded in a deep committed spiritual revolution. I see no justice in the post-Nietzschean world, I see no Overman, unless we acknowledge this source of will to power in Being, and I am now convinced of one thing, that Being, the Being of the philosophers, is not just an idea, but is Real. Being is the Named. Of that I am convinced. Being has a name and it is known. And it is recognized and strength is drawn from it and when we finally bow down to the One Being not in religion but in truth, not under priesthood but under conviction of the truth, then this force will rejuvenate the world, just in time. As you know I am anti-utopian, but that does not mean that I am a pessimist. We are on the other side of the madness of Nietzsche. We are fighting for the new sanity. The price of our survival is to sweep away the deadly poison of usury that has grown over the ruins of our Germanic civilization and built its plastic palaces and its elegant post-modernist museums to our once vibrant culture. The struggle for survival has come back to its guardians and they must do their duty. The German people must awaken in themselves again their spirit as it was awakened by Luther, and Goethe and Schiller, and Kant and Hegel, and Bach and the indomitable Beethoven. Is it wrong to believe in the spiritual heritage of people who have produced men such as these and our warriors? I do not feel any shame for our fighting men, wronged for a century. We must prepare now for the future. We must educate the guardians.

'Well, as you can see I am still young at heart, simple and clear in my convictions. Forgive me. What of me? I know only one thing. I must serve this great cause and work for this end. This heroic task needs no music – but it needs knowledge and it needs men and women ready to serve. I feel, to tell you the truth, that my life far from being nearly over, is just beginning. And so my friend, I must say goodbye to you, but do not be concerned about me whatever you may read or hear.

'We embark on tomorrow with a great optimism, God willing.'

A NOTE ON THE TYPE

This book was set in Garamond, which is based
on types first cut by Claude Garamond (c. 1480–
1561). Garamond was a pupil of Geoffroy Tory
and is believed to have followed the Venetian
models, although he introduced a number of
important differences, and it is to him that we
owe the letter we now know as "old style". He
gave his letters a certain elegance and feeling of
movement that won their creator an immediate
reputation and the patronage of Francis I of
France.